CRUEL CANDY

A COZY CORGI MYSTERY

MILDRED ABBOTT

CRUEL CANDY

Mildred Abbott

for
Nancy Drew
Phryne Fisher
and
Julia South

Cover, Logo, Chapter Heading Designer: A.J. Corza - SeeingStatic.com

Main Editor: Desi Chapman

2nd Editor: Corrine Harris

Recipe and photo provided by: Rolling Pin Bakery, Denver, Co. - RollingPinBakeshop.com

Visit Mildred's Webpage: MildredAbbott.com

❀ Created with Vellum

"Oh, Watson, what have I gotten us into?" I stared at the shop through the safety of my car window. It was smaller than I remembered. I leaned forward, bumping my forehead on the glass. Fairly tall, though, at least two storeys. With the dark-stained log siding and forest-green trim and shutters, it looked like a log cabin had been sandwiched between the other stores of Estes Park.

And it was mine.

The thought ushered in a wave of excitement. A tingle of nausea too, but more excitement than anything. At least that was what I told myself.

The death grip I had on the steering wheel of my Mini Cooper said otherwise. I tore my gaze away and turned a forced smile toward the passenger seat. I needed to be brave for Watson.

He arched a brow lazily at me, not bothering to lift his head from his curled-up position. Managing to pull one of my hands free from the steering wheel, I slipped the car into Park, then scratched behind his pointed fox-like ears.

"We're here. It's been a long day, and you've been a great copilot." A grumpy copilot, but that was normal for Watson. A quality that probably wouldn't be as endearing if he wasn't so stinking cute. "I'd say you deserve a treat. What do you think?"

At what was unquestionably his favorite word, Watson bounded to a standing position and began bouncing on his two front legs. His stubby corgi legs didn't make him that much taller, though the bouncing helped.

"And this is why we work, you and me. Food is king, behind books, of course." I snagged a dog bone out of the glove compartment, started to request for Watson to sit first—demands never worked—then decided it wasn't worth the effort, and held it out to him. Despite his voracious appetite, which even a shark would envy, Watson avoided removing my fingers and made short work of the snack.

After a couple of minutes, Watson cocked that judgmental brow of his once more. His thoughts were clear: *The prolonged staring is creepy, lady. But I'll forgive you for another treat.*

He had a point. I was putting off the inevitable.

Which was silly. I was excited, happy. Time to launch into an adventure.

I turned toward the shop again, took a breath, and opened the car door. *Here goes nothing.*

My knees popped as I stepped onto the sidewalk, and I sucked in a breath at the tweak in my back. I supposed a drive halfway across the country was a reasonable excuse, even if I was still two years away from forty. I glanced back at Watson, who had curled back into a ball. "Seriously? The ten-hour nap wasn't enough?"

After a few more seconds of glaring, Watson acquiesced, stood, and stretched. He raised his knobbed-tail of a butt in the air, just letting me know he was still in charge, and then leisurely crossed the console and hopped out beside me.

"Thanks for joining me, your highness." I shut the car door and looked up at the shop. It seemed a little larger once I stood in front of it. It would be charming. My gaze flicked to the sign above the door that read *Heads and Tails*. *Would* being the operative word. Who knew what horrors lay behind the papered-over windows. I'd never envisioned a behind-the-scenes look at a taxidermy business, but it seemed I hadn't been aware of a lot about my future. Well, whatever. If it was too horrible, I'd just pay one of those junk companies to come in and haul everything away.

That thought brought a sense of relief, but then another swept it away. I was thinking like a city girl. I doubted a town the size of Estes Park had a junk-removal business.

And again, I decided, whatever.

I had a feeling I was going to be saying that a lot.

Movement caught my eye from the store window to the left of my shop. Before I could make out a figure, I was captured by the crimson script over the glass, *Sinful Bites*.

Perfect. Some fortification would be needed in the very likely chance I was getting ready to walk into a store filled with petrified dead animals. I veered off to the left, giving a quick pat to my thigh. "Come on, Watson. Mama deserves a—" I almost said treat. "—reward too."

A pleasant chime sounded as I opened the door to Sinful Bites and allowed Watson to waddle through. I cast a quick glance around. The store was done in my favorite colors—the walls, cabinets, and displays all in various shades of rich earth tones. It felt homey, comfortable. Exactly what I would be going for when I redid the god-awful taxidermy shop. That boded well for my relationship with my neighbor.

A woman with short, spiraling brunette hair looked up in surprise from behind the cash register. Her brown gaze glanced at me in confusion, then moved to the front door, and back.

I offered a hesitant smile, feeling like I'd messed up somehow. "Everything okay?"

"Yes!" The woman smiled back, wide and bright. "I'm so sorry. We just closed. I could've sworn I locked the door," she said, her tone apologetic.

"Oh. Well, I can come back another time." Despite myself, I couldn't keep my gaze from traveling over the gleaming cases filled with candy.

"Not at all! My fault for not locking the door, and I haven't started putting things away yet, so I insist." Another smile.

"Thank you. I promise I'll be quick." I moved closer to the cases, unsure if I would be able to keep that promise. Though slightly picked over, the display was magnificent. Gleaming fruit tarts in golden brown crusts, hand-size brownies filled with nuts, caramel, and chunks of candy. Fudge of every flavor, truffles of various shapes and colors, and chocolate. So much chocolate that I was suddenly aware I'd smelled it since I walked in the door. No wonder I felt at home. Chocolates done in nearly every imaginable way—almond bark and turtles, covering pretzels, marzipan and nougat.

Heaven, I decided. I'd died and gone to heaven. I managed to tear my gaze away from the smorgasbord of delights and look at the woman. "I think I'm in love."

The woman chuckled good-naturedly and held out her hand. "I'm Katie. Always nice to meet someone who appreciates dessert more than cardio."

I stiffened for a heartbeat, wondering if I should be insulted. But at the twinkling of Katie's eyes, I couldn't help but laugh. I felt an instant kinship with the woman. "Yes, I'll take dessert any day over fitting into a size eight. Though my real weakness is carbs, not candy. Give me a hot loaf of fresh bread and I can die a happy woman." I took Katie's hand.

"Me too, actually. I might work in a candy shop, but bread is what I do best."

"Then I am definitely glad to meet you, Katie." I released her grip and gestured down to Watson, who stared up at me, salivating. "My little corgi friend is Watson, and I'm—"

"I'm telling you, Lois, if you would just use actual sugar in your baking instead of all the stupid substitutions—" Two elderly women walked through the back door of the shop, cutting me off. They both halted at the sight of Watson and me. The blonde cast a quick glare at Katie. "I thought we closed."

Katie flushed. "I apparently didn't lock the door. Sorry. But I believe—" It seemed she was searching for my name. "—our friend here is in need of some chocolate."

The blonde looked at me and cast another glare down at Watson, but by the time she met my gaze once more, her smile was wide, even if it didn't reach her eyes. "Well, of course! You've come to the right place. Sinful Bites has the best chocolate in town."

The other woman's eyes narrowed, but she didn't say anything.

Katie cleared her throat, cutting the brief tension that had filled the place. "Do you know what you'd like? If you're not sure, I can get you a sample."

Getting-to-know-you time was most definitely over. Which was doubly sad, as at any other time I would've taken Katie up on the offer of samples. Under the inspection of the blonde, however, I didn't dare. "You know, I just drove into town, and I really should get home. Why don't you give me an assortment of the ones you like best." Chances were high such a thing would end up being more expensive than I'd intended to spend on candy, but since I was going to be neighbors with the shop, it was clear I needed to put my best foot forward as quickly as possible.

"Home?" The third woman finally spoke. "Do you live here? You must be new in town. I don't think I've seen you around."

"I just moved in. Quite literally, in fact." I smiled at the woman, who seemed nicer than the blonde. "I've visited several times. I have family who live here." I nodded at Katie as I spoke, trying to include her again and continue the introductions. "I'm Fred, and this is Watson. We just made the long drive from Kansas City to Colorado. This was our first stop in town."

The woman gave a chuckle. "Fred? I don't believe I've ever met a woman named Fred." She gestured to herself and the blonde. "I'm Lois Garble, and this is my sister, Opal. Opal owns this candy shop, and I own the one two doors down, Healthy Delights."

"It's a pleasure to meet you both." *Sisters?* The two women definitely didn't look like sisters. Although, now that I thought about it, they had the same features. It was only everything else that was different. Lois had naturally graying hair, a clean and wrinkled face, and she wore a plain cotton dress.

Opal had dyed, highly stylized blonde hair, copious amounts of makeup, a brightly colored dress, and tons of jewelry. "My true name is Winifred Page, but everyone calls me Fred."

"Well, I think that is simply adorable. And it suits you." Lois shrugged playfully. "Like I said, I've never met a woman named Fred, but if I could imagine one, she'd have beautiful auburn hair just like yours. I've always thought Opal would look ravishing in that color." She cast a sidelong glance toward her sister's coiffed blonde hairdo.

Opal didn't comment about becoming a redhead. "Page? Your last name is Page, and you have family in town? I don't remember a family with that name."

I nodded, though for some reason I was tempted to lie. "Yes. My mother grew up here. Phyllis Oswald, though now she's Phyllis Adams."

Both Katie and Lois seemed to take a step back, but Opal didn't budge, instead folding her arms over her ample bosom. Any semblance of welcome or friendliness vanished, not that there'd been much from Opal. "I thought I'd heard your name before." If looks could kill. "So that means you're the one taking over Sid's taxidermy shop."

Again, lying seemed the intelligent thing to do. "Yes. Though I won't be doing taxidermy. I'm going to be changing it to a bookshop. It's going to be called the Cozy—"

"I'm sorry, but we're closed." Opal sniffed, nostrils flared. "And for future reference, I don't allow dogs in my business."

I halted, unsure what to say. One of the things I'd always liked about the town was Estes Park's dog-friendly nature. I started to glance at Katie and then thought better of it. The last thing I wanted to do was get the shopgirl in trouble. I gestured back toward the door. "Sorry for...." What was I sorry for exactly? "Watson and I will just be going."

Lois gave a loud good-natured laugh and swatted playfully at Opal, which Opal avoided with a glare. "Please forgive my sister. It's her intake of sugar and butter and things the good Lord never intended us to eat. It makes her cranky." She managed to deliver the line with a cheerful air, making it sound more like an endearing quality than an insult. Lois headed around the counter and slipped a birdlike arm through mine. "You come with me. I'll get you some sweets that are natural and nourishing, and I have homemade dog-bone biscuits." She looked down at Watson, then back at me. "I didn't notice. How adorable. He's a redhead like you." Without waiting for a response, she looked back down once more.

"What do you say... Watson, was it? Do you want a treat?"

Watson bounced on his two front paws again at the word, causing Lois to chuckle. The only thing I really wanted to do at that point was get away, but Watson's reaction settled it. Plus, how could I deny the woman without seeming rude?

I allowed myself to be led toward the front door and cast a glance back, offering a quick smile to Katie and a final apologetic grimace to Opal.

Lois led me out of the shop, around the front of Heads and Tails, then pulled out her keys to usher me into Healthy Delights. "Sorry, I already shut the place down, but I'll get you an assortment of things from the back. Give me one second, dear." She flicked on the lights and then headed through the back door to disappear with a small wave.

The tingle of nausea rose again. My shop sat directly between these two sisters. Lois seemed sweet enough, but Lord knew what I was getting myself into with these two. Pushing the thought away, I spared a glance at Lois's store. It was the exact same layout as Opal's, just flipped, but the similarities stopped there. Where Opal's candy shop felt cozy, warm, and friendly—despite the woman herself—Lois's was done in a garish combination of pastel colors, sickeningly sweet pinks, and yellows. My stomach gurgled.

Watson didn't seem to notice. He chuffed and looked up at me.

"Your treat is coming. Calm down." I shook my finger at him. "And I blame you for pulling me into this."

He chuffed again, and this time bounded so his paws landed on my foot, clearly telling me to shut up and get on with the treat giving.

"You're ridiculous." As if watching a car crash, I looked back at the shop. It didn't make any sense at all. How could the sister who owned the cozy and delicious-smelling candy shop be so irritable, while the one who designed the monstrosity that looked like Easter on speed was the kind one?

Before the color palette had a chance to permanently scar my corneas, Lois returned with a large brown bag in one hand and a massive dog bone in the other. "I'm sorry I have to rush. I'd love to get to know you and your precious pup, but Opal and I have dinner plans, and I don't want to keep her waiting." She thrust the bag into my grip. "For future reference, I make everything Opal does, just a healthy, all-natural version. It's fun to mix and match."

I forced a smile. I hadn't been able to identify what smell seemed to linger in the air, but it wasn't pleasant. If the desserts were edible, I'd be shocked. "Thank you. I appreciate your kindness. I'm sorry if I did anything to offend—"

Lois waved me off, whipping the dog bone in the air, a large crumb flying across the room. In a rare show of speed, Watson zoomed away in pursuit. Lois didn't seem to notice. "Never you mind. That's just how Opal is. You see, she and I were hoping to purchase the taxidermy shop after Sid passed, but your mother wouldn't consider selling. Said her daughter was taking it over." Though her chipper tone didn't fade, Lois's smile did, a touch. "I won't hold that against you, dear." Another hand pat. "But if you decide you want to sell, we'd appreciate it if you would let us know." Leaning closer, her voice dropped to a whisper. "Lots of people move to Estes Park, captured by its beauty and charm, only to discover they feel a little trapped in the mountains and constricted by small-town life. Chances are it will happen to you too. Of course, I hope not, but"— and yet another pat—"when it does, remember my sister and me."

I opened my mouth to respond, but was utterly at a loss for words.

Words didn't seem to be required. Lois wrapped her arm around my shoulders, which was no small feat, considering I was several inches taller than the woman, and led me toward the door. She shoved what was left of the dog bone at me. "This is made from peanut butter I ground myself, and organic grains. They are five dollars apiece, but this one's on the house." She opened the door for me and stood aside. "Welcome to town, Fred."

"Thank you, Lois." I clutched the paper bag and waggled the dog bone in Watson's direction, capturing his attention. "Come on, buddy. Let's go." Watson tore off from where he'd been sniffing in the back corner of the shop. I nodded my thanks to Lois once more, then walked to the car. I changed my mind a few paces away from my burnt-orange Mini Cooper. Turning around, I headed back toward the front door of the taxidermy shop. I'd been so excited to see inside, to get lost in the planning of what my bookstore would look like, that I had driven straight here when we got into town.

After locking her front door, Lois crossed in front of Heads and Tails, gave a final friendly wave, and disappeared into Sinful Bites once more.

Pushing the odd sisters out of my mind, I addressed Watson as we stopped at the front door.

"I'm sure you'll love all the smells you're going to find in there, but just remember, if we come across a dead animal and I scream, you're forbidden from telling anyone. If you do, there won't be any treats for a week."

Watson gave a quick, sharp bark.

"Crap. I said treat, didn't I?" At the repeated word, Watson resumed bouncing, his dark brown eyes wild with excitement and looking like a deranged bunny.

I couldn't help but chuckle as I lifted what was left of the dog bone. "Luckily, we have one. You can get it as soon we're inside."

I paused at the lockbox hanging from the door handle, then set the bag of healthy candy—*what a thought that was*—at my feet. Catching my reflection in the window, the paper behind the glass causing it to act nearly as effectively as a mirror, I couldn't help but scowl. My hair was a complete mess, and a sheen of light caught the gleam from dog hair. I glanced down at my peasant blouse. Life with a corgi meant I was in constant need of a lint roller, but after the day in the car, things had gotten to a nearly ludicrous level. To make matters worse, I gave my brown broomstick skirt a flick with my wrist and sent a fresh wave of dog hair spiraling around me. Wonderful. So much for putting my best foot forward. Meeting three of my neighbors while looking like I was part corgi myself.

Well, whatever. Too late to be helped now. Besides, it wasn't like I'd ever actually be dog-hair-free anyway. Pushing the concern away, I pulled out my cell and scrolled through text messages from my mother until I came across the lockbox code. I punched in the four digits and gave a yank. There was no click and the lock didn't budge. Clearing it, I tried again. Same reaction. I checked the text, confirming I had the numbers right, then tried a third time. When I was still denied, I tapped my mother's name and lifted the phone to my ear.

It rang several times, then finally clicked to a message saying my mother's voice mail was full and could no longer accept messages. What else was new? I tried the lockbox one final time. For a moment, I considered breaking the window on the front door and reaching in. It was my shop, after all.

What a way to start a new adventure, breaking and entering. Patience had never been a virtue I fostered, but letting out a resigned huff that sounded more like a corgi than a woman, I stuffed my cell back into my pocket. "Looks like we're thwarted at the moment, Watson."

Retrieving the paper bag, I led us back to the car, held the door for Watson to hop in, then followed.

I'd been so ecstatic about opening the bookshop, I hadn't even considered who my neighbors might be. Being directly between Lois and Opal was going to be.... Well, I was afraid I didn't have a word for exactly what that was going to be. I doubted it would be all that pleasant.

Watson chuffed.

"You feel it too, don't you, boy? Who knows what we're going to have to face with those two. At least we have each other."

He let out a long pitiful whine.

"Aww, look at you being all empathetic. What's gotten into—"

I realized Watson's frantic gaze was focused on my hand, not looking deep into my eyes and sharing a moment. "Oh, I forgot." I handed him what remained of the all-natural dog biscuit with a sigh.

When the combination on the front door of the cabin didn't work either, I had half a mind to leave the bag of all-natural candy on the porch for the squirrels, toss Watson into the Mini Cooper, and hightail it back to Missouri. Or anywhere else, for that matter. As far as hitting the Reset button of life, this was turning out to not be so smooth.

This time, however, Mom answered her cell on the third ring. I sat on the ancient driftwood bench while Watson plopped down on the corner of the porch and observed a couple of chipmunks scampering over the roots of a nearby evergreen.

Though only a little after six in the evening, night had fallen, and the November air was brisk. As we sat waiting, my impromptu uprooting of my entire existence began to feel right once more. I'd forgotten how vibrant the stars seemed in the mountains, overlooking rocky peaks and massive forests.

They were so clear a person could almost believe she could reach out and pluck one from the sky. Even the swirls of the Milky Way were visible. Not to be outdone, the soft breeze whispered gently through the bare branches of aspen trees, carrying the fresh scent of pine, earth, and snow. The gurgling of the partially frozen Fall River, several yards away from the back of the cabin, was nearly hypnotic.

This was good. So very, very good.

I'd forgotten how beautiful it was in Estes Park. Forgotten the way my pulse slowed and my mind relaxed. It didn't matter that the bookshop would have a cranky candy-store owner on one side and a fake candy store on the other.

After nearly ten minutes, I also realized I'd forgotten just how far removed my grandparents' old cabin was. There was a new development of designer houses to drive through to reach it, but they were a good quarter mile away and not visible through the trees. At any other time, that would be a pleasing thought, but not when I couldn't get into the house. My grandfather always said bears were more afraid of us than we were of them. I never wanted to test his theory.

Just as my brain began to turn the sounds of the surrounding forest into something sinister and I was about to suggest to Watson that we take refuge in the Mini Cooper, headlights cut through the trees, flashing across the porch and then disappearing again as a vehicle came up the winding road.

The massive truck barely missed my rear bumper and slammed to a halt. Mom practically threw herself out of the passenger side, giving a graceful leap to the ground, which, considering her diminutive stature and age, was impressive.

"Winifred!" She hurried across the small distance, met me before I'd made it off the porch, and wrapped me in her arms. "Welcome home, baby!"

"Hi, Mom." As always, at barely five foot tall, she felt like a doll in my embrace, so tiny and fragile.

She pulled back after little more than a moment, then scurried over to the front door and began punching what seemed like random codes into the lockbox. "Come on. Let's get you inside. You must be freezing. You're not used to these Colorado winters."

"You've only been back six years, Mom. Surely you haven't forgotten that Midwest winters are much worse than anything you all have out here."

Watson bounded up and let out a happy yip, then rushed toward the truck.

"Well, hello there, little buddy." Barry Adams leaned his tall lanky frame down to rub briskly at

Watson's sides. "Good to see you again." They'd only met two other times, but for whatever reason, they'd bonded. Each time Watson saw Barry, it was like Barry was a walking dog bone. After a few seconds, Barry stood once more and gave me a tentative hug. Despite that hesitation, his deep voice was warm and full of affection. "Glad you're here, Fred. Your mother's been over the moon knowing you are going to be near once more. And I think you'll be happy."

I returned his hug. I liked the guy. A lot. Not to the same level as Watson, but still. However, it was odd to think of him as my stepfather now, so I didn't. "Thanks, Barry. I think it'll be good."

"Barry!" Mom called out, not bothering to look over her shoulder nor pausing in her frantic pushing of buttons. "Do you remember the combination I put on this?"

"Pretty sure you put the key in your pocket, didn't you?" He winked at me.

Mom threw up her hands and then shoved one deep into her pocket. "Sure enough! I swear, I don't know how I manage to remember a thing." She slid the key into the lock, twisted, and threw open the door. Then she turned and handed me the key. "I guess this is yours now. Don't worry about the lockbox. I'm sure the combination will come back to me at some point."

And then the four of us bustled in. Mom and Barry made quick trips around the house, flicking on lights.

Watson looked up at me, his tongue hanging out in a grin.

"Go on." I waved him off. "Go explore."

He was gone, nose to the ground and snuffling here and there like he was guaranteed to discover a treasure.

After shutting the door, I glanced around the cabin. It was smaller than I remembered—probably eight hundred square feet. But also cuter than I recalled. Most of the furniture needed replacing, but the design was good, and the log walls and beams crossing overhead gleamed golden in the light. I peered into the kitchen. It hadn't been updated since the sixties, but my grandmother had kept it in pristine condition until she died. It seemed the renters over the past decade had done the same. I liked the mint green of the refrigerator and the oven. It suited me.

"We came out here yesterday and cleaned a little. It wasn't in too bad a shape. We were hoping to have time to clean out the shop as well, but we didn't quite get around to that." Mom stroked the curtains over the small kitchen window, like she was petting Watson. "I found the time to make these yesterday, though. I thought the kitchen needed some freshening up."

I stepped forward, narrowing my eyes. "Are those flamingos?"

Mom nodded. "Sure are. I think the pink makes the kitchen look happy."

"I hope you like them." Barry shrugged good-naturedly. "I picked out the material."

"I couldn't tell." I had to stifle a laugh. The background of the flamingo material was a lemon-yellow and lime-green tie-dye print. Other than at his and Mom's wedding, I had never seen Barry out of his tie-dyed T-shirts and loose-fitting yoga pants. "They are lovely. Thank you."

He beamed.

"Well, we would've done more, but we didn't expect you for another six weeks." Mom turned back from the curtains, concern etched over her face. "I thought the agreement was for you to stay at the publishing house for the transition to go smoothly."

The room suddenly felt hot. "I changed the agreement." The last thing I wanted to talk about was Mysteries Incorporated.

Mom swiped a lock of long silver hair behind her ear as she crossed the kitchen and took my hand into hers. There were still streaks of auburn in her hair, the last vestige of the only physical trait I'd inherited from her.

"I know what she did was awful, honey, but Charlotte was your best friend since you two were little. I'd hate for a little thing like money and business to come between you."

My mother could find the good in a rabid wolverine if given the chance. "Don't worry about Charlotte. Trust me, she's not worrying about us." Mom opened her mouth to protest, so I switched the topic as I turned to Barry. "I met the neighbors. I don't think Opal was thrilled at my arrival."

Barry groaned. "She is a piece of work. If I had other property I could give you besides the taxidermy shop, I'd do it in a heartbeat so you wouldn't have to put up with her every day."

Mom swatted him. "None of that. Opal's a fine woman. Sure, she may be a little grumpy at times, but she's got a heart of gold. Everyone knows that Lois's business would've had to close its doors within a couple of weeks if not for Opal. Sinful Bites has supported Healthy Delights since they opened. Anyone who's willing to do that for their sister can't be all bad."

I sucked in a little breath before Barry could protest. "Oh, I forgot. Lois gave me a bag of candy. I left it on the porch. I better go get that."

"Probably a good idea to leave it right where it is, dear." Mom offered a guilty smile.

"It's really that bad, huh?"

They both nodded. It was Barry who found the positive that time. "But Lois is a fine woman. Couldn't ask for nicer."

Mom smacked the counter. "That reminds me. I made Tofurky stew. It's in the car. I'll be right back. I figured you'd be famished after your drive. I wish Verona and Zelda weren't on a cruise. We could've had our first family dinner."

We stared after her as she hurried away. Barry grinned at me awkwardly. Several silent moments passed before Watson pattered in, accepted a pat on the head from Barry, and then settled at my feet.

Barry cleared his throat. "You like the flamingos, huh?"

"Barry!" Before I had to lie another time, Mom's raised voice drifted in through the front door of the cabin. "Where did you put the stew?"

He flinched, scrunched up his face in concentration, then his watery blue eyes grew large. "Oh, crud. I forgot she asked me to put it in the truck." He grimaced. "Be right back."

I couldn't help but smile after him. I'd always held my mother and father's relationship up as the perfect marriage. They'd balanced each other out. Mom was flighty, forgetful, and fun. Dad had been serious, kind, and brave. I had to admit, Mom and Barry together? They didn't balance each other out in the slightest; they were nearly two identical peas in a pod. But happy. So very happy. I loved that my mother got to have two good marriages in her lifetime when most of us couldn't even find one.

Mom poked her head in through the front door. "Seems like you and Watson are coming to our house for dinner this evening." She plopped the paper bag from Lois just inside the doorway. "Here, in case you get a desperate craving in the middle of the night."

THREE

Sleep didn't come easily, which was no great surprise. I'd left Kansas City in such a rush that I'd dropped a small fortune for a moving and packing company to do it all for me and then drive everything out later. The delivery date was still two weeks away. A long time not to have my own bed, but the sense of freedom of hitting that Reset button was more than worth tossing and turning for a while. Between the lumpy mattress and excitement over starting on the shop, a full eight hours wasn't in the cards. I doubted I'd even gotten five.

As a result, I poured nearly half a pot of freshly brewed coffee into a large thermos, coaxed a bleary-eyed Watson to the car, and drove downtown before the sun had even considered coming up.

Mom never remembered the code she'd used for the lockboxes, but she'd given me eight different keys off her ring, swearing that one of them would be the correct one. Chances were low, but this whole move was about hope, so I decided to latch on to that as I parked in front of Heads and Tails, sparing a glare at the awful wooden sign above the door. "That will be the first thing to go, Watson. Disgusting name, considering." I winked at him. "The Cozy Corgi is much better, don't you think?"

Watson didn't even bother to sigh.

"You're no fun."

After managing to convince Watson to leave the warmth of the car, I stood in front of the shop door, trying key after key. By the fifth failure, hope was fleeting. As I tried to decide if I would drive directly to Mom's and wake her up so I could get her whole ring of keys, the seventh key slid in with ease, then produced a little click as I twisted the door handle.

Look at that—hope paid off. Removing the key, I unlocked the deadbolt, then paused. This was it. I was about to see my future bookshop for the first time, enter the place I hoped would bring fulfillment and meaning back into my life.

I cracked the door, and Watson stiffened to instant alert, shoving his nose into the narrow opening.

His reaction startled me, but it only took a second to remember what the store was. Currently my dream future was filled with stuffed, dead animals. Maybe I should've waited for daylight.

Watson pushed against the door, shoving his muzzle in.

"At least one of us is going to enjoy this." I opened the door, and Watson rushed through. "Remember our deal. If I scream, it's our secret."

He didn't bother to reply. With the windows covered in paper, no glow from the streetlamps illuminated the place, and I felt around on the wall beside the door until my fingers found the light switch. Taking a steadying breath, I flicked it on and looked around.

For a ridiculous moment, I wondered if I was in the wrong shop. There was a large central area, with smaller rooms on all sides, so I couldn't see everything, but from what was visible, there wasn't a taxidermic animal in sight. Furniture and cabinets here and there, but not even a solitary furry creature. Letting out a sigh of relief, I stepped all the way in and shut the door. Watson's claws clattering over the hardwood floor sounded from somewhere in the back.

I started to walk in farther, then paused, pulled a tie out of my pocket, and twisted my hair into a quick ponytail. I might not see any animals, yet, but the place was filthy. The last thing I needed was spiders getting in my hair.

I moved through the rooms, flicking light switch after light switch. With each room I entered, my excitement grew. I might be sandwiched between Opal and Lois, for better or worse, but this little shop was everything I'd hoped for and more.

At least it would be.

Barry had mentioned the shop had been designed as a little house ages ago and had never been renovated to a more open concept, which would better suit a store. I had planned to hire a construction team to remedy that. As I explored, I changed my mind. Each room was connected to the other, surrounding the central area. All I needed to do was take off the doors. Each room could have a different theme. Kids' books in one room, cookbooks in another, romance, mysteries—every genre would have its place.

My entire goal for the shop had been to create a warm, inviting environment where people could not only shop for books but also hang out and enjoy reading them. A cozy sanctuary from the rest of the world, tucked away in an adorable tourist trap of a mountain town. This was turning out even better than I'd envisioned. A couple of the rooms even had fireplaces in the corners. I could get a few mismatched armchairs and sofas to spread around. The Cozy Corgi was going to be something special.

Near the rear of the main room, a beautiful wooden staircase led up to the second floor. I could just make out the spindled banister running around the circumference. I knew the previous renter had lived up there, and I hadn't decided if I was going to rent it out or make it part of the bookshop. Probably would have to use it for storage and inventory.

From Watson's reactions, it was easy to tell where the taxidermy had been. He was especially interested in the corners of the rooms, sniffing around, then looking up the wall as if he could see what had been there. In most of the places, I could just make out an imprint in the dust where something had hung. The previous tenant had passed away in the summer, and the shop had stayed empty. I could've sworn Mom and Barry said they hadn't had a chance to do anything to the place, what with my moving the date up so suddenly, but maybe they had just been referring to a deep clean. Finding it all in good shape was a nice surprise. Deep cleaning I could handle myself. Trying to figure out what to do with mounted bears, foxes, cougars, and Lord knew what else would have been a completely different story.

There were two closed doors at the back of the shop. I opened the first one, and flicked on the light to reveal a bathroom much in need of updating. I checked to see if the toilet worked; it did, a good sign. The other room opened into a tiny storage space—not nearly enough for what a bookstore would require. Which only reinforced the possibility that upstairs would need to be used for storage. Just as I started to close the door, Watson barged in, continuing his sniffing exploration. He made his way around the circumference of the room, then paused at what appeared to be a small deep freezer in the corner.

He stuffed his nose between the wall and the back of the deep freezer, then shoved against it with a wiggle of his butt. With a whine, his attempts grew more frantic.

Something about his reaction caused my skin to prickle into gooseflesh. "Come on, boy. Let's check out the upstairs."

Watson looked over his haunch at me, let out another whine, and returned to pushing against the deep freezer.

Feeling like the first victim in a slasher film, I

crossed the room and stood in front of the appliance. I was being ridiculous. If anything, the freezer was probably just full of meat which Watson could smell.

The sensation of being nervous about a deep freezer overrode feeling like the dumb bimbo in a horror movie. I threw open the lid with a flourish just to get it over with and move on, then glanced inside.

Two huge black eyes gleamed up at me from the darkness. With a scream, I released the lid and practically threw myself backward. It shut with a bang.

With all the commotion, Watson let out a startled yelp and rushed past me.

I nearly turned tail and follow him out of the storeroom but couldn't rip my gaze away from the deep freezer. What had I just seen? An animal, obviously. I was in a taxidermy shop, for crying out loud. Granted, I didn't know they put animals in deep freezers, but I supposed that made sense. Those eyes, however, were unlike anything I'd ever seen.

It was an animal. Right? Had to be. I didn't need to look at it again to figure that out.

I turned to leave the room again and found Watson staring at me warily from the doorway. "Well, you were absolutely no help."

With a sniff, he padded back into the room and returned to sniffing at the base of the deep freezer.

He managed to get his head all the way behind it—apparently slamming the lid had moved it a few inches from the wall. He let out a growl, wriggled his butt some more, and then popped back out, looking the epitome of satisfied.

Watson was nearly out the door again when I realized he had something in his mouth. Without thinking, I reached down and snagged it, fearing it could be poisonous or harmful.

It wasn't. Just a feather. Angling it toward the light, I gave it a twist. It was a soft brown with white spots across it.

Watson growled softly.

I looked down to find him glaring up at me. "Not for you, buddy. Sorry." His gaze remained focused on the feather, so I stuffed it in my jacket pocket, hoping it would be out of sight and out of mind. "We'll go get you another of those dog bones when Healthy Delights opens later this morning."

He didn't seem impressed.

I looked over at the deep freezer once more, a strange sense of dread wriggling in my gut. "Oh, for crying out loud." I was being ridiculous, again. Reminding myself that I was a self-made business-woman and the daughter of a cop, I stomped back over to the deep freezer. I paused long enough to pull out my cell phone and flick on the flashlight. With another steadying breath, I opened the lid and angled the light inside. This time, I didn't make a noise, but was still unable to repress a shudder.

A large owl stared up at me.

Just an owl.

Nothing dangerous or even all that surprising. I supposed when Barry and Mom got rid of all the other taxidermy, they hadn't thought to check the deep freezer. Though who in their right mind would? You expect to find dinner or ice cream in a deep freezer, not whole animals. Though the owl was frozen, obviously, I couldn't quite tear myself away from its gaze. Even in death, its eyes were huge and gleaming.

Behind me, Watson growled again.

It was enough to break the spell. I closed the lid, softly this time, and turned to Watson. He started to head back to the deep freezer, but I scooped him up. It always surprised me how heavy the little guy was. "No way! We're getting out of this room, shutting the door, and neither one of us is coming in here until I find someone to do whatever you're supposed to do with dead owls."

Watson hated to be carried, and he thrashed in my arms until I placed him on the floor outside the storeroom. He continued his reproachful glare as I shut the door. Letting me know just how over me he truly was, Watson waddled into the main room, cast a dismissive glance in my direction, and galloped up the stairs.

The second floor. Crap. Maybe Sid What's-his-name had several deep freezers filled with animals upstairs.

Might as well get it over with.

Keeping the light on my cell phone on, I walked up the wide staircase. To my surprise, the steps were in good shape, not even a creak. I found the light switch easily enough and turned off the flashlight and stuffed my cell phone away once again, then looked around. The upstairs was the same size as the first level, but here the layout was open concept, like a studio apartment. Sid's old bed, sofa, and entertainment center spread out in different clusters. Against the north wall were two separate rooms. The first one stood open and revealed another bathroom. The second door was closed, and Watson lay happily in front of it, knob of a tail wagging as he chomped down on something.

"Seriously? Again?" I hurried over to him and attempted to pull whatever it was out of his mouth. He jerked away and shuffled back several feet. From his deepened glare, it was clear I'd be getting attitude from him for my rudeness for the next several days. At my feet, where he'd been, were two pieces of wrapped candy, and an empty piece of ripped cellophane. I scooped them up and inspected them. They were round and hard, almost looking like gumballs except for their deep black color. I sniffed one to make sure it wasn't chocolate. Although in that small quantity I doubted it would hurt Watson if he managed to eat one. Even as I thought it, I could hear him crunching on the piece he'd successfully gotten out of the wrapper. The scent was instantly recognizable. Licorice.

I pocketed the candy as well, simply to get it out of the way, and gave Watson a glare of my own. "Never mind. I don't see a large all-natural dog bone in your future today, after all." At least it hadn't been chocolate. I loved Watson, but his food obsession drove me nuts. He refused to eat dry dog food of any kind, yet absolutely anything we found out in the world was surprisingly edible—even if it wasn't.

Deciding not to do battle to try to get what remained of the licorice out of his mouth, I opened the door, flicked on the lights, and stepped into a large kitchen.

The floor was littered with candy. More of the

hard licorice scattered among pieces of chocolate, marzipan, and peppermints. An overturned pan of brownies was scattered across the countertop. A cardboard box was stuffed with something, and another was overturned, spilling out a variety of copper cookie cutters.

Something brushed against the hem of my skirt, causing me to jump, and I looked down to see Watson sneak past me into the room.

"Oh no you don't. No more candy for you." I started to reach down to scoop him back up, but he let out a low, dangerous growl.

I flinched back. I'd only heard that growl, which sounded surprisingly vicious, a few times, both occasions when some stranger was at the door. He'd never growled at me like that.

It took me a moment to realize he still wasn't growling at me. His front shoulders were drooped down and his back was rigid, rump in the air as he showed his fangs. He crept toward the counter, still growling.

For the second time that morning, gooseflesh broke out over my arms. This time, however, as I followed him, I felt even more like the first victim in a horror movie.

As Watson rounded the corner, he sank lower, his growl deepening.

At his feet was a large wooden rolling pin, the end of which was stained a dark red.

I moved a little farther in to see behind the L-shaped counter, and sucked in a breath.

Opal Garble lay on her side, between the counter and a metal island laden with cooking supplies. She was in a deep-purple bathrobe, her perfectly coiffed blonde hair spread out on the floor in a pool of blood.

It was rare that another woman could make me feel small. Truth be told, it was rare that a man could make me feel small, but next to Officer Susan Green, I might as well have been a petite waif. Though I'd inherited my father's strong build, adding my own softness and curves to the equation, Officer Green was every ounce as sturdily built as I was. But she looked like she spent every weekend carrying boulders up the side of the mountains. In addition to her girth, she matched my five-foot-ten height, and her gaze leveled with my own. Her pale blue eyes were narrowed and hard.

"You're the one who called in the murder, correct, Ms.—" She glanced at her notepad. "—Page?"

"Yes, that's right." The floorboards above our heads squeaked, and I glanced up. At least three officers were taking care of Opal, while Officer Green stayed with me. She didn't seem overly happy with the arrangement. "I'm the only one here, well, me and Watson." I motioned down to where Watson lay at my feet, his muzzle resting between his stretched-out front paws.

Officer Green made another note without looking at Watson and spoke as she wrote. "Why exactly were you here?"

"I'm opening a bookshop."

"In Heads and Tails?"

I nodded. "Yes, though it will be called the Cozy Corgi."

She lifted her pen and cocked her head at me. "I was under the impression Opal and Lois Garble were going to take over the lease and expand their businesses." It wasn't a question.

"Honestly, I wasn't aware of their desire to do that until I met them when I got into town yesterday afternoon."

"You just moved to Estes Park?"

"Yes, ma'am." The police officer had to be a good ten years younger than me, but being deferential seemed the best way to go.

Impossibly, her gaze grew colder. "Let me get this straight. You're telling me that you just moved in from out of town, and yet you managed to snag the lease of a coveted piece of property away from two local women who've lived here their entire lives? One of whom is now lying dead above our heads."

Again I glanced toward the ceiling. I could almost hear Opal applauding the accusatory tone in the officer's voice. "Well, this piece of property is owned by my mother and stepfather, so...." I licked my lips. "I didn't know anyone was interested in the property when I decided to move out here. My step-father is a native as well, and my mother was born here, though she only moved back fairly recently."

It seemed having native ties to the town was important, though I wasn't quite sure why I shared all that information. It wasn't like I had done anything wrong, even if Officer Green seemed to think differently.

And it appeared I'd only scratched the surface of how cold both her gaze and her tone could become. "Your stepfather is Barry Adams?"

Suddenly I wanted to lie. It wasn't a sensation I was used to, but since driving into town, it was starting to feel like a habit. "Yes, ma'am."

"And your mother is Phyllis Adams?"

I nodded.

She rolled her eyes. "Of course. Well, that explains a lot."

"It does?"

"Yes. It does." She scribbled some more notes. "My brother owns the magic shop."

I waited for an explanation of that statement, then realized none was coming. I also realized I probably didn't need one. Barry had inherited a ton of property from his family. My mother helped him manage them. They were both wonderful people, and I loved them dearly, but I often pitied their tenants. Despite their good intentions, I was certain that forgetting the code on a lockbox and not knowing which key opened the door was the tip of the iceberg of what their management style was like.

The officer checked her watch, appearing to do some mental calculations before speaking again. "You reported that you got here around five in the morning?"

I nodded again. "Yes, ma'am."

"You can call me Officer Green."

"Yes, ma'am." I shook my head, wondering if I was intentionally trying to channel my mother in that moment. "Sorry. Yes, Officer Green."

She grimaced. "And yet you called dispatch over an hour later. What took you so long to report the death?"

"I called less than five minutes after I discovered

Opal. Probably less than three." I gestured around the shop. "Watson and I were inspecting the place. Making renovation plans and how to lay out the bookshop."

She cocked an eyebrow. "Watson?"

I pointed down at my feet.

"Oh." Another eye roll. "Is your dog a master of renovations, or just a literary scholar?"

"Neither, I'm afraid." The officer wasn't a dog person, obviously. Why wasn't that a surprise? "He did discover an owl."

"An owl?"

This time I pointed toward the back room. "In the deep freezer. There's an owl. Watson found it." What was wrong with me?

"Miss Page, a beloved member of the town has been murdered in your shop. Do you really think I have any concerns about an owl?"

"No, ma'am—err... Officer Green." I needed five minutes to clear my head, maybe then I could stop answering questions like a maniac. No, actually, breakfast. I needed breakfast.

She let out a long-suffering sigh, then leveled her stare at me once more. "And where were you before arriving here this morning?"

"At my house. Sleeping." I almost added that it

wasn't so much sleeping as trying to sleep, but then reminded myself that I didn't need to ramble incessantly. And that I needed to get ahold of myself, hungry and tired or not. Very few people made me nervous. It was ridiculous that I was allowing Officer Green to get to me. Though, I rationalized, it wasn't every day I stumbled across a dead body. I supposed I was allowed to be little thrown off.

"Can anyone confirm that?"

I pointed at my feet again.

She glanced down at Watson and then returned to her notepad. "Okay then." She scribbled something, then opened her mouth to speak again, but the sound of footsteps on the stairs caught her attention.

I followed her gaze and managed to keep my jaw from going slack. It was a testament to just how overwhelmed I'd been at the sight of Opal that I'd somehow missed this police officer, who carried a briefcase, coming into the shop. At well over six feet tall, he looked like he'd just stepped off the set of some television police drama. I placed him at around forty years old. His stunningly handsome face was all sharp angles and chiseled features. From the way his body moved beneath his uniform, it seemed the chiseling kept going below his neck.

I kicked myself mentally. There was a dead

woman upstairs. The last thing I needed to notice was how handsome one of the police officers was. Or that his swept back raven-black hair made him look like an old-time movie star. On top of all that, the last thing I needed or wanted in my life was another man.

He flashed a smile at Officer Green which didn't meet his eyes, and then his bright green gaze flicked my way. He appeared to halt for a heartbeat, his gaze making a quick trip down my body, then back up, and then his smile did meet his eyes. "You must be Ms. Page. You made the initial call, correct?"

"Yes, that's true." Look at that. I *could* speak. And do so without drooling. "My name is Fred."

This time, when he halted a few feet away, his pause was more obvious. His eyes narrowed, but it seemed more out of curiosity than anything. "Fred?"

"Winifred Page, Sergeant." Officer Green's eye roll could literally be heard in her voice. "She's the daughter of Barry and Phyllis Adams."

I started to correct her, but the sergeant stepped up to us and held out his hand for Officer Green's notes.

She gave them over reluctantly, a slight blush rising to her cheeks. Anger, I thought. Not embarrassment.

He flipped through before handing them back. "Thank you, Officer. If you'd help the others, I'll take over with Ms. Page."

For a moment, it looked like she was going to argue, but then she cast an accusatory glance my way. "Yes, sir." She stomped off.

He held out his hand to me. "I'm Sergeant Branson Wexler. Nice to meet you... Fred." A wry smile played at the corner of his lips. "Though I'm sorry it's under these circumstances."

Though his tone stayed professional, I was certain he was flirting. Which was ridiculous. Men like him didn't flirt with women like me. Maybe one more symptom of skipping breakfast.

Granted, he was several inches taller than me, but men like him wanted the blonde bombshell or dark-haired maven. And if they took a walk on the wild side, it would be for the redhead vixen type. Not the curly redhead bookworm. I took his hand, offering him a firm shake. "Nice to meet you as well, Sergeant."

He held my hand for just a moment too long. Long enough to confirm the lack of breakfast had nothing to do with what was happening between us.

Maybe just an interrogation technique?

He motioned toward the counter in the main

room. "I noticed some chairs in there. Care to have a seat?"

"Sure. Thank you." I started to head that way, but the sound of his masculine gasp caused me to pause.

"And who's this?" Sergeant Wexler squatted down and extended the back of his hand to Watson, who gave a tentative sniff, then cocked his head, allowing his ears to be scratched.

Not instant love, but not revulsion either. From Watson, it was almost a ringing endorsement.

"This is Watson. He's a corgi." I wasn't sure why that second detail was needed. Nor was I sure what was wrong with me. I'd gone from nervous with Officer Green to completely flustered with Sergeant Wexler.

And who was I kidding? I knew exactly what was wrong with me.

His smile was genuine, and his gaze stayed on Watson as he stretched out his other hand to offer further scratches. "Watson, huh? Like the little guy who helped out Sherlock Holmes?"

"Yes, exactly. He...." I started to tell him where Watson's name had come from, but for some reason held back. It seemed too personal, considering I'd just met the man. No matter how attractive he was, or that he was making my pulse do stupid things.

After a few more seconds, Watson pulled away, and Sergeant Wexler let out a chuckle. "He's not exactly the cuddly type, is he?"

"Depends on the moment."

He stood. "I suppose the scene of a murder isn't exactly cuddle time." He tipped an imaginary hat toward Watson. "Good call, sir." Then he motioned back toward the main room and smiled at me again. "Shall we?"

We took seats in some folding chairs that were behind the counter. Sergeant Wexler took out a yellow legal pad from his case and placed it on the counter as he scrawled a quick note across the top. "I know you just went through this with Officer Green, but I like to hear things for myself when I can." He paused in his writing and met my gaze once more. Though still friendly, any hints of flirtation had vanished, and he was all business. It put me more at ease. Probably a sad commentary that official police interrogations were easier to handle than possible flirting. "Care to walk me through how you found the body?"

"Certainly." I folded my hands in my lap and decided to give him the quick version. He could ask more questions if needed. "Watson and I came to check out the store. I'm converting it to a bookshop, so I wanted to get an idea of what work I have to do. When we made our way upstairs, that's where I found Opal. Well, where Watson found Opal, actually. I saw the bloody rolling pin and then saw her. I think I probably stared at her in shock for a few minutes, and then I called 911."

As he wrote, he nodded a few times, then looked up again with the next question. "Did you touch anything when you went in? Accidentally knock over the candy or check for a pulse?"

I shook my head. "No. She was very clearly dead. And the room was like that already. Candy everywhere. It was what we found first. Or what Watson found first. There were a few pieces of candy outside the door, and he snagged one before I could get to it." I dug in my pockets and pulled out the two wrapped pieces of candy. The feather fell on the floor, but I snagged it before Watson could get it and shoved it back into my pocket. I held out the candy to Sergeant Wexler. He took them and lifted them to his face for inspection. "You said you found these *outside* the door?"

"Yes."

"The door to the kitchen was closed when you

and Watson went upstairs?" He looked at me over the candy. "These two pieces were on the floor outside the door, and then you went in and found Opal?"

"Yes." I nodded. "Actually there were three pieces, Watson ate one of them."

The corner of his lips quirked into a brief smile, and he made another note. "Any idea what Opal Garble was doing in your shop?"

"No, I...." I sat up a little straighter. In all the hysteria, that question hadn't even entered my mind. Probably because the store didn't feel like mine yet. That and considering it was my first time walking in on a dead body, I probably wasn't thinking too clearly. "I have no idea. Although, it looks like she was baking or...." I thought of the boxes. "Packing?"

"Yes, it definitely seems that way. Strange that she would be cooking here. Obviously I've never inspected it, but I would assume Sinful Bites has its own kitchen. Any thoughts of why Opal would need to bake in your kitchen?" Sergeant Wexler's tone wasn't accusatory or dismissive like Officer Green's had been, but there was definitely a different feel to it now. I couldn't quite put my finger on what it was.

"Like I said to the other officer, I just got into town yesterday. And I've only met Opal once. And this morning was my first time to ever walk into the shop. I wouldn't have been able to tell you what the kitchen even looked like, or where it was, much less why someone was using it."

"But your father and mother own this property, correct?"

"Yes. Though Barry is my stepfather. My father passed away several years ago."

His expression softened for a moment. "Sorry for your loss."

I nodded but didn't offer anything else.

"Do you think your stepfather or your mother were allowing Opal to rent the space for extra cooking room or something?"

"I don't—" I cut off my explanation. Somehow, answering Officer Green's questions had been easier, despite her obvious dislike. Sergeant Wexler's charm and good looks were throwing me off, which was frustrating. I didn't care how charming and good-looking the man was. I wasn't going to say anything incriminating about my stepfather if I could keep from it, not that I had the slightest worry that Barry would do such a thing. The man refused to even use mousetraps, let alone bludgeon an old woman with a rolling pin. Nevertheless, I wasn't going to offer up that he hadn't cared for Opal Garble.

"Not that I know of. It was their idea that I open the bookshop at this location. Granted, I arrived a few weeks earlier than I'd intended, but they'd made it very clear the shop had been vacant since the previous tenant's death."

"Very well, then. Thank you." Another note. "I'll need to speak to them, of course. Do you have their number handy? If not, I'm certain I can get it easily."

"Of course." I pulled out my cell to retrieve their numbers. There was no reason not to give him those.

Before I could answer, another police officer approached. "Sergeant, I think you'll want to see this."

"I'm in the middle of questioning a witness, Officer Jackson. Give me a moment please." His tone was dismissive, almost arrogant, and at odds with how he'd spoken to me.

The other policeman hesitated and then motioned over his shoulder. "Sorry, sir. But we found something rather important in the basement."

There was a basement?

"Is there another body, officer?" Again, Wexler seemed irritated to be interrupted.

"No, sir."

"Then please give us—"

"The basement is a grow house, sir. A large one."

Sergeant Wexler sat up straight, and I gasped. Both he and the other policeman looked at me. His green eyes showed surprise. "You know what a grow house is, Fred?"

I nodded. "Yes. An illegal marijuana-growing operation."

More surprise, and this time obvious suspicion.

At the look, I figured a little more explanation was in order. "My father was a detective. One of the cases he was working on was bringing down an illegal drug ring." The last case he worked on. The one that had gotten him killed.

As Sergeant Wexler got up to follow the other officer, I stood as well. We'd taken a couple of steps before he looked back at me, a thick, perfectly shaped brow cocked, and an air of amusement in his tone. "And where do you think you're going?"

I hesitated. "To the basement...." As the words left my lips, I knew it was ridiculous. Of course I wouldn't be allowed to go.

"Did you already know about the basement, Fred?" He turned toward me fully, his professional demeanor back in place. "Did Watson sniff that out as well?"

I shook my head. "No. He's typically on the search for food, not drugs."

Sergeant Wexler's lips twitched once more. "I'll make sure to document that in my notes, just so suspicion doesn't fall on your corgi." There was that flirtatious tone again.

The officer who'd discovered the basement snorted out a little laugh. "I doubt he would smell it, especially if he wasn't trained for such smells. The room seems to be extremely well insulated."

When Wexler spoke again, any hint of flirtation was gone. "Be that as it may, I'm afraid I'll have to ask you and Watson to stay up here."

I started to nod, then a wave of claustrophobia seemed to wash over me. "Actually...." I motioned toward the front door. "Do you mind if I get some fresh air? I need to get out of here for a little bit."

He hesitated, considered, then smiled. "Of course, but don't go anywhere, please."

"I'll stay right outside."

He gave another nod and then followed the other policeman to the back of the store.

I didn't bother to look down at Watson, just patted my thigh and headed toward the door. "Come on, boy."

I blinked as we stepped outside, the sunlight hurting my eyes after hours in the dim shop. I checked my watch. Nearly eight in the morning. The other stores were opening, and though it was winter season, a few tourists already wandered the sidewalks, most of them pausing to inspect the police cruisers in front of the shop, then glancing at me.

I considered going back inside to avoid the curious looks, but the thought made my skin crawl. Instead I leaned against the wall of the shop and folded my arms, trying to look unapproachable.

Now that I was outside in the brisk November air, the strangeness of the situation became more pronounced. There was a dead woman in the top floor of my soon-to-be bookshop. A murdered, dead woman. And as if that wasn't enough, a marijuana-growing operation was in the basement.

How had Mom and Barry not noticed it when they'd removed the taxidermy? Although, knowing them, they wouldn't have thought to check a basement. Who knew if they were even aware they owned a basement.

A basement! What a nice thought. I wouldn't have to use the top level for storage after all. I realized I was smiling and then shook my head. Dear Lord. I couldn't allow myself to be that awful. Being happy about a basement when a woman had lost her life? Although, I supposed it was okay to try to find a bright side. I glanced at Watson who was staring up at me. "Don't look at me like that, Judgy."

At the sound of the door opening beside my right shoulder, I jumped and turned around to see someone looking up at me.

"Fred!"

It took me a second to put a name to the pretty round face. "Katie, hi." I glanced behind her into the interior of Sinful Bites. The cases were still filled with candy and sweets. My stomach rumbled. Then I recalled that the owner of Sinful Bites was currently getting a chalk outline above us.

"I didn't realize you were here. Do you know what's going on with all the cop cars?" Katie stepped fully outside. "I arrived about fifteen minutes ago. They were already here."

"Yes, unfortunately I do. I hate to—" Katie's words sank in and I paused. "You just got here?"

She nodded, looking confused.

"Don't most bakers have to get up in the wee hours of the morning to get the day's treats prepared?"

Watson whined, causing Katie and I to look down. He lifted a paw.

"Oh, I said the word, didn't I?" I reached down offering an apologetic pat. "Sorry, boy." I grinned at Katie. "I said the T-word."

"I caught that." Katie sighed, her demeanor shifting to something like annoyance. "And you're right. Most bakers do exactly that, and if it was my shop, that's what I'd do as well. But Opal doesn't like me to come in outside of business hours. I'm supposed to do the baking in between customers during the day. She's very strict about the times I can be here." Katie attempted to look over my shoulder, though it didn't do her any good, considering the windows were still papered over. "The police are in your shop?"

"Yes."

Katie looked up at me expectantly, waiting for an explanation. "Are you okay?"

"I'm fine. Thank you." We stood awkwardly for a few moments while I considered what to do. I was certain I shouldn't tell her anything, but it felt strange to know her boss was dead inside my shop and to just stand out here and pretend everything was normal. I glanced around, making sure no tourists were nearby, and lowered my voice. "Actually, Katie. I'm sorry to tell you this, but...." I swallowed. Crap. What was I doing? I'd never had to break the news of anyone's death before. Although now I'd started, I couldn't think of a way to finish without simply telling the truth. "It seems that... Opal was killed in my store this morning. Or last night. I'm not really sure which."

"Opal was...." Katie took a step back and

bumped into the doorframe. She shook her head as if to clear it. "Are you serious?"

"Yes. I'm sorry."

"Opal is dead." Katie shook her head again, then repeated the phrase. "Opal is dead." Her brown gaze flicked up to me. "Killed, you said? As in... murder?"

I nodded, something about Katie's reaction seemed off.

"Wow." Katie blinked a couple of times, her voice seeming far away. "Wow. Murdered. That's really... wow." She glanced back into Sinful Bites and cocked her head. "Huh. Maybe that means...." Her words trailed off, so I didn't get to hear what that might mean, and when she looked back, there was a blush over her cheeks. "Sorry. That's awful. About Opal."

I couldn't keep from saying, "You don't seem all that upset."

She let out a snort and a half laugh, though it was a dark sound. "You have to forgive me." She gave a little shrug. "I tend to be blunt. And that can throw people off sometimes. But no, I'm not all that upset. Surprised, definitely. Upset? No. Opal wasn't a very nice woman. Wasn't a very nice boss either."

"Yeah, I noticed that yesterday."

Katie's eyes widened at my words.

"Well, I did." I gave a shrug of my own. "I tend to be blunt myself, most of the time." Growing up with a father who was a detective, death wasn't a new topic in my world. Not that he shared his cases with me that much, but he'd never been one to live by the notion that a person shouldn't speak ill of the dead.

Something passed between Katie and I, an understanding perhaps. Once more, I felt the kinship with the woman that I'd sensed the day before. "I'm sure this is absolutely horrible, but I've been up since before dawn, and with all the drama, I haven't had a chance to eat anything. I think my blood sugar is crashing. Any chance you have something more substantial than chocolate in there?"

She beamed. "I do! I have this amazing ham-and-cheese roll that I baked at home last night. I brought it for my lunch. But you can have it if you want. Opal never lets me bake things like that for the store."

"Oh my God, you're a godsend!" I glanced back toward the front door of my bookshop, hesitating. Whatever. I wasn't under arrest, and I wasn't exactly wandering off. I was right next door. And I needed breakfast and to get out of the cold.

Katie hung up the Closed sign and warmed up the roll.

Despite myself, I was unable to keep from making almost embarrassing sex noises as I ate it. And not just because I was ravenous. The thing was pure perfection. A stunning combination of buttery, flaky crust, salty ham, and creamy cheese. Proving just how much I loved Watson, for every two bites I took, I ripped off a piece and tossed it to him. He seemed to enjoy it as much as I did. "Katie, what are you doing working in a candy shop? You need your own bakery."

"Tell me about it. I've been trying—"

At that moment, a door slammed somewhere in the back room, and a second later, Lois Garble stepped into the doorway, her long gray hair wild and her eyes wide. She looked between Katie and me, and when she spoke, I could hear the fear in her voice. "Have either of you seen Opal? She wasn't at home when I woke up. And then I get here to find police cars outside."

Katie and I looked at each other. "Why don't you sit down, sweetie?" The tone and gentleness Katie used when she addressed Lois made it clear she held completely different feelings for the owner of Healthy Delights than she had for the woman's sister. "We need to tell you something."

· · ·

"I swear, Mom, it was one of the hardest things I've ever had to witness." Watson and I were snuggled together on the couch in Mom and Barry's living room. "Lois completely broke. Screaming, crying. She was hysterical."

"It makes sense." Barry gave a serious nod. "Not only were they sisters, but Opal did everything for Lois. Everything. From managing the money to handling conflict. Not that there was much conflict with Lois, with as gentle as she is. I don't know how she'll cope without Opal."

"She'll be fine." Mom's soft voice seemed miles away, as did her expression as she stared unfocused over my shoulder. "It's amazing the pain a person can go through and survive. How we keep living even when our world crumbles." Again I couldn't help but notice how small Mom was. She'd always been petite, a trait that had gotten squashed by my father's genes, but she seemed more and more fragile.

Barry reached across the coffee table and squeezed her hand, then held it gently.

I knew the moment Mom was reliving. Over the course of the afternoon, I'd relived it several times myself. It hadn't hit me when I'd seen Opal's body, not during the interview with the police, not when I told Katie. But Lois's reaction? I'd seen it before. I'd been with Mom the night the officers came to our door about Dad.

She was right. I wouldn't have guessed Mom would've survived with how broken she was. Much less that she'd move back to her childhood home and marry her childhood sweetheart barely a year later.

The afternoon had drained me. I was beyond exhausted. I had no doubt any sleep I'd missed the night before would be more than made up for the second my head hit the pillow. I didn't plan on setting my alarm.

"They're not letting me back into the shop for several days. They're not sure how long. Though that's not surprising, considering the shop is the scene of a homicide and a secret drug den." I stroked Watson's back, and he let out a long, contented sigh. "Not a great beginning for a place I was going to call the Cozy Corgi. There's not much cozy about murder and drugs."

Mom smiled, seeming to come back to the moment. "Chances are it'll make your opening week so much more successful. I guarantee you everyone will want to drop by, probably take a bunch of pictures and post them online with some murder-hashtag thingy."

"Murder-hashtag thingy?" I chuckled softly, the laughter relaxing me a bit.

"You know, that social media stuff. They use hashtags. Personally I can't stand Twitter, too much drama. But Instagram is fun. Although I don't use too many hashtags on my posts."

Look at my nearly seventy-year-old mom being hip. "I didn't know you had an Instagram account."

"Oh, sure. Verona and Zelda got me going on it. It's a lot of fun. Mainly I just post pictures of the jewelry I make, but sometimes I post about the grandkids on there."

I could just imagine Barry's twins trying to teach Mom how to use social media, I wished I'd been a fly on the wall.

Barry smirked. "Remember that time you accidentally posted the naked picture of me? You nearly lost your account."

Mom rolled her eyes and gave me an exasperated sigh. "I was simply doing it to use the filters. They really do make a picture a thousand times better." She patted Barry's hand. "Not that you need filters, of course." She looked back at me. "I swear, in this day and age you'd think this country would be a little less puritanical. Half the world has a penis. I'm not sure what the big deal is."

"No. No, no, no." I waved my hands in front of my face, letting out a sound that was somewhere between a scream and a laugh. "It's enough that I had to walk in on a dead body today. I cannot handle these mental pictures on top of it all."

"Does that mean you don't want to see the photo your mother and I took this morning? We're sending it out next month as a Christmas card. We're both wearing Santa hats." Barry couldn't keep the smile off his face. "*Only* Santa hats."

"Argh!" I waved my hands again. "I swear you're trying to kill me. Please tell me you're kidding."

Barry opened his mouth, but I cut him off.

"On second thought, don't answer that. It's better not to know. And please take me off your Christmas card mailing list."

Barry shrugged. "Fine. No Christmas card for you." He focused on Watson. "But you will get one, won't you, buddy? You don't want to be left out on Christmas."

At attention from Barry, Watson leapt off the couch and hurried over to get petted.

The place where he'd lain against my thighs suddenly felt cold.

As the two of them had a love fest, Mom turned back to me. "On the bright side, now that you're not going into the store for a few days, we can spend the time getting the house together. I know your things aren't scheduled to arrive for a couple more weeks, but I'll help you do some cleaning, and maybe we could go shopping for some new items before your stuff gets here. Start fresh."

Though it killed me to think about postponing getting the bookshop ready, she had a good point. It would be nice to get the house done as much as we could. "I don't think we need to do much shopping. This house is so much smaller than what I had in Kansas City. I'll be getting rid of a good two-thirds of what I own as it is."

She fluttered her hand in dismissal. "I already said I thought you should leave it all there to begin with. Why you would want anything in your house that Garrett touched is beyond me. There's no reason to bring that negative energy all the way to Colorado."

"Why are you doing this to me? What have I ever done to you?" I rubbed my temples. "First Opal's dead body this morning, then I'm scarred with images of you and Barry engaging in a dirty Christmas photo shoot, and now you bring up my ex-husband."

"What? I'm just saying that there's only so much

healing that sage and crystals can accomplish." Mom shrugged. "But if you don't want a fresh start, that's your choice. I'll bring over the crystals and sage anyway."

I latched on to the subject change, more out of desperation than anything. "Speaking of a fresh start, I really appreciate you guys handling the taxidermy. I can't tell you how much I was dreading walking into all those dead animals."

Mom and Barry exchanged looks, and then both turned back to me. Mom stared at me quizzically. "What do you mean, dear?"

I wasn't sure how to answer that. "Well, just what I said. Thank you for handling cleaning the bookstore out. I wasn't sure what I was going to do with the taxidermy that—" I had to recall the man's name. "—Sid had left."

Barry shook his head slowly. "We told you, darling. We hadn't made it down to the shop. We barely had time to pick up at your place and hang the curtains."

I studied them like they were playing the world's most boring, unfunny joke. "Are you serious? You didn't get rid of all the taxidermy?"

They both shook their heads again, and Mom

answered this time. "No. You're saying it wasn't there when you went in this morning?"

Before I could answer, a loud knock sounded at the door.

The three of us jumped, and Watson ran to the door, letting out a vicious bark.

Barry stood with a groan and chuckled. "I swear, as long as a potential robber never sees that little guy in advance, you've got yourself one hell of a guard dog." He walked across the room, patted Watson on the head, and opened the door.

Mom and I leaned around to look, and I sucked in a little gasp at the sight of Sergeant Wexler illuminated in the doorway.

He glanced into the house, gave a little wince and a nod as his gaze met mine, and then refocused on Barry. "Mr. Adams?"

Barry nodded. "Yes, sir. What can I do for you?"

Again Sergeant Wexler grimaced. "Sorry to say, but I need you to come with me to the station for questioning in regards to Opal Garble's murder."

SIX

If it hadn't been clear that I'd moved to a small village of a town, sitting with Mom at the police station clarified it instantly. The times I'd visited Dad at the station in Kansas City, the place had been a madhouse, bustling with activity, noise, and chaos. In the middle of it, stood my father—tall, strong, capable of handling anything that came his way.

As we sat waiting for some word, the little police department in Estes Park was nearly as quiet as a hospital waiting room, save for the ringing of phones. There was even one of those inspirational posters of a cat hanging on a branch that was in classrooms when I'd been in school. From the yellowed tattered edges, I figured it was about how long the poster had hung on the wall. If not for the officers in uniform, I probably wouldn't have been able to identify where we were.

Mom kept her hand in mine, forcing me to

acknowledge how much more frail she had grown over the past six years. I'd noticed on our visits, but I was shocked that her skin was paper thin, and the bones underneath felt as fragile as a sparrow's. She looked at me with red-rimmed eyes.

"This is taking forever. It's ridiculous. Like Barry could ever kill anyone."

I squeezed her fingers. "We've been on the other side of this a million times, Mom. I'm sure it's just protocol." I spared a glance at the open box of dough-nuts on the counter. They'd disappeared gradually as we'd sat waiting. "Things don't seem to be in a hurry here." Nor did they seem to care about stereotypes or leaving their snacks in a break room.

"I can't imagine what they possibly could've found linking it to Barry. We haven't even been in that shop since Sid died. I doubt we've been in it for a couple of years before that, actually."

"Probably best not to speculate. We'll get our answer soon enough." I attempted to keep my tone neutral, even though I wasn't sure why I bothered. "However, it would probably be best to call someone other than Gerald Jackson. I know he and Barry go back to childhood—"

"There's no point discussing it, Fred." Mom cut me off, and there was a touch of steel in her exhausted tone. "Gerald, Barry, and I all go back to childhood, and there's no one else Barry would consider representing him. No one."

"But Gerald? Seriously, Mom? Can you imagine what dad would—" At the sting in her eyes, I shut up. Not the time.

Actually, it was the time. The only time, but bringing Dad into it wasn't going to help.

There was movement down the hall that caught my attention. Officer Green. I was surprised to see her still on the clock. I started to call out to her but then thought better of it. She'd made her feelings about Barry and Mom very clear.

Maybe she was the reason Barry had gotten pulled into this.

Thankfully, she didn't notice us and walked out of sight. As I was getting ready to return my attention to Mom, and come up with some other argument about Gerald, Sergeant Wexler stepped into the hallway, sipping something out of a Styrofoam cup. The sight of him brought a flash of anger and a sense of betrayal. Even as the emotion cut through me, I was aware it was preposterous. We didn't know each other. He hadn't betrayed me. Still, I went with it. I spared Mom a glance. "I'll be right back."

She followed my gaze and nodded. "Finally.

Thank you, dear. You and your father were always better at handling things like this."

It took an effort not to bring up Dad in terms of Gerald again, but I called out to Sergeant Wexler halfway down the hallway and realized the loud echo was coming from me stomping. I slowed, forcing calm into my voice as I approached him. "May I speak with you?"

He hesitated. And I could see some sort of struggle in his beautiful green eyes. *Beautiful green eyes?* The thought only managed to increase my irritation.

"I'm sorry, Ms. Page, but I'm not quite ready to speak to you and your mother yet." He offered a smile, one that I was certain he practiced and used with every family he encountered. Handsome, measured, and cool. My irritation sparked further.

"Then let us see Barry. I'm sure he's a wreck, and it would definitely help my mother."

"Ms. Page, I know you aren't aware of how all this works, but trust me—"

"My name is Fred, not Ms. Page." Even as I hissed out the words, I was aware that no matter what he said, I would've been annoyed. If he'd called me Fred, I'd probably have taken his head off and told him to call me Ms. Page. But I didn't care. "And maybe you haven't been told, but my father was a police detective. Rest assured my mother and I are well aware of how all this works. And I know, especially with as slow as things are around here, you can expedite this if you had half a mind. The very idea that Barry is involved in this is absolutely ludicrous. Anyone who's spent more than two seconds with the man would know that. The fact that you're considering his involvement only shows how incompetent you must be."

Well, that was a dumb move. It was rare that my temper got the best of me, but his handsome face was making me want to bash it into the wall. Or kiss it. Which made me want to bash it even harder.

To my surprise, when he spoke, he didn't sound offended. "Barry Adams was a police detective? I don't think we're speaking about the same man, *Fred*. I might not have lived in Estes Park very long, but I'm fairly certain that detail wouldn't have escaped my attention." Not only did he not sound offended, but if anything, there was an amused twinkle in his eyes. Which was also irritating.

"See, right there. I gave you this information earlier today. Barry is my stepfather, not my dad. Obviously if you can't keep such a simple detail straight, it explains how you could accuse Barry of something so absurd." In the back of my mind, I knew my father would turn me over his knee to hear me speak to another police officer that way. That or die laughing.

Sergeant Wexler's annoyingly twinkling eyes studied me, as one of his stupidly charming grins formed at the corner of his lips. Finally he motioned with his cup to an empty room next to us. "Well then, by all means, why don't you let me know how to do my job."

I stepped in, waited for him to shut the door, and took a place by the table. I was not going to sit down. "First off, I don't appreciate the sarcasm, Sergeant Wexler."

Yep, full-blown grin. "Branson, please."

"What?"

He shrugged one of his shoulders. "You're the one who insisted we be on a first-name basis, so the name's Branson."

I stared at him. "Are you actually flirting with me right now?" Those words I *hadn't* meant to say.

He opened his mouth to speak, then gave another shrug. "I'm not in control of how you interpret my words, Fred."

I gripped the edge of the table. It didn't wobble. Bolted down, it seemed. Probably best for both of us.

I took a calming breath, at least it was supposed to be calming. My temper wasn't going to help Barry.

"What in the world do you have on my stepfather? I don't actually think you're incompetent. I was impressed with your skills today." I figured I'd get more with flattery than anger. And as much as I hated to admit it, I had been impressed with him. "You can't possibly think Barry killed Opal Garble. I don't believe you'd make such a stupid mistake."

"It seems you're the master of the compliment and insult combination." He took a sip of his drink, his grin never faltering. "And since your father was a detective, you're obviously aware I can't share that information with you. You also know I wouldn't bring him in if I didn't have cause."

I did. It didn't make sense, but he was right, mostly, and I knew it. "You can hold him for twenty-four hours without any real cause. It happens sometimes, when the police don't have any real leads but it makes it look like they're doing something."

His grin finally faded. "And that was pure insult. I can promise you, Fred, I am not that kind of cop. I'm good at what I do." His eyes narrowed. "I will let you know, considering the information I do have, I will be keeping your stepfather overnight."

I balked, and guilt bit at me. Sometimes my

temper helped; other times it made matters worse. "Don't do that just because you feel insulted by me. It's beneath you."

"Obviously we don't know each other." He took a couple of steps toward me. Considering the glower on his face, I supposed I should feel threatened, but I didn't. I did feel something, however, even if I didn't want to admit what it was. He held my gaze before continuing. "I can assure you, your critique on my professionalism and skills have nothing to do with why I'm holding your stepfather overnight."

Probably five minutes too late, I opted for keeping my mouth shut. I didn't want to make matters worse than I already had. And strangely, I believed him. He wasn't simply trying to prove a point. As nonsensical as it was, he'd found some connection.

When I didn't speak, Branson's posture relaxed and his tone softened. "I am sorry for what you and your mother are going through. Especially considering you're part of the police family."

His sincerity was clear, and it dampened my anger somewhat. "Thank you." I cleared my throat. "I'm sorry for letting my temper get the better of me."

"I have to admit, I'm a bit surprised that with

your connection to how things work that your family has chosen Gerald Jackson." Actual concern laced his voice. "I'll happily call you a better lawyer. You could open the yellow pages, close your eyes, and pick one at random and get a better lawyer."

Tell me about it. "Gerald and Barry are old friends." I attempted to infuse some confidence in my tone. "Barry has complete faith in his abilities."

His eyes narrowed. "Then why isn't Gerald having this conversation with me right now?"

"He stepped out to get a kombucha. He needed some energy." I wanted to crawl in a hole. "Some natural energy."

He smirked, considered for a moment, then nodded to himself. To my surprise, he let the topic of Barry's choice of legal representation drop. "Here's what I can do. Why don't you get your mom, and I'll bring Barry in." He pointed toward the mirror. "I'll be listening in of course." His green eyes twinkled again as he cocked that perfectly shaped brow. "I can trust you to stay away from funny business, right?"

"Unfortunately I didn't come prepared with a nail file. I think we're good this time." To my surprise, I heard the tenor of laughter in my voice. "And thank you. I appreciate you allowing us to speak to him."

"If you want to wait for your lawyer, then—"

We probably should. Gerald might be able to make it where we could have a private conversation, but, I doubted it. We'd be waiting for nothing.

He studied me a bit longer, his smile changing and softening yet again. He started to speak, then stopped with a shake of his head and took a step back. "Get your mom. I'll be right back."

Mom burst into tears as soon as Branson shut the door, leaving Barry with us. She wrapped her arms around Barry and shook.

I didn't resent Barry. Nor had I ever had any feelings of betrayal that Mom had married him so soon after my father's passing. However, sometimes I wondered whether Dad's death affected Mom less than it did me. Seeing her now took any notion of that away. She'd always been flighty and silly and tender. But she'd also been a cop's wife. There wasn't much she couldn't handle. This wasn't the same woman who'd raised me.

For his part, Barry's eyes were also red-rimmed, and his hands trembled as he smoothed her hair. "It's okay, my dear. It's okay."

I gave them a minute or two, then patted the metal table in the center of the room. "I don't know how much time Branson—Sergeant Wexler is giving us. So let's talk." I waited for Mom and Barry to shuffle over and take seats beside each other, their fingers remaining intertwined. Then I leveled my gaze on Barry. "Trust me, I know you had absolutely nothing to do with this, but I also believe the police have something on you. They wouldn't be keeping you overnight if they didn't."

Mom sucked in a breath and gripped Barry's hands tighter. "They're keeping you overnight?"

Barry turned to me. "They are?"

"Yes. Sorry, but they are." Well, crap, I could've handled that better. "They might not have told you that yet, though I'm certain they've informed you on why they are holding you on Opal's murder. What in the world is going on, Barry?"

He glanced between Mom and me. I swore I could see the guilt in his eyes grow as he looked at Mom. My gut twisted.

Apparently Mom could see it too. "Barry?" Her voice trembled. "Surely you didn't have anything to do with this?"

"Of course not. I would never hurt anyone. Even Opal."

I cast a fleeting glance toward the two-way mirror, though I'd promised myself I'd give Branson the impression I didn't care that he was listening in.

Mom relaxed, already convinced. As was I. I couldn't picture Barry hurting anyone. But neither could I imagine him having that tone regarding anyone who'd just been murdered. There was definitely something there.

I reached out and tapped his arm, holding his attention. "Fill us in."

Again guilt crossed his face, and he lowered his gaze. "You're not gonna like this. And I'm sorry."

Mom flinched but didn't pull her hand away— some of her old resolve showing through. "Then tell me already and get it over with. Whatever it is, we can't deal with it until we're all on the same page."

"Why don't we wait for Gerald. He can't be much longer. He might be able to make it where we have a bit more privacy before we get into this." Another glance towards the mirror. "How hard is it to find kombucha?"

Barry turned wide eyes on me. "He makes his own. He probably had to drive out to Glen Haven. He actually lives across the stream from Verona and Zelda."

Of course he'd live by my stepsisters in a place without cell reception. And of course he'd have to drive all the way there to get his homebrew when Barry needed him. I started to suggest waiting, but really, what was the point? Like Gerald could do anything, even with all natural energy coursing through his veins. "Fine. Go ahead."

I could swear I heard Branson laughing behind the glass.

Barry nodded, then took a long slow breath before launching into a story. "Opal had a side business of making edibles." He fluttered his free hand. "Edibles are baked goods or candy with pot in them. Marijuana."

"You know Charles was a detective in the drug enforcement unit. I'm well aware of what an edible is, Barry." Though she still didn't pull her hand away, Mom's voice was hard. "You also know how I feel about drug use."

"I know. I'm sorry. That's part of why I've never told you." His eyes widened, and he rushed ahead. "And I promise that's all I do. Just some edibles to help me sleep at night. I'm not addicted to heroin, or meth, or anything like that."

Mom rolled her eyes. "I know that, stupid. You mean to tell me you've been using edibles in our house?"

He nodded. "I'm so sorry. I—"

I tapped the table. "Guys, focus. You can figure that out later. What does this have to do with Opal's murder? How does consuming edibles get you arrested? I thought pot was legal in Colorado."

Mom shook her head. "Not in Estes Park. They still don't allow it to be sold."

"But is it legal to use it here?"

They both nodded.

I glared at Barry. "Are you telling me you were selling it? You became a drug dealer?" Maybe we should've waited for Gerald.

Mom gasped, and Barry shook his head emphatically. "No! Never! I just bought edibles from Opal. Or at least I used to." He grimaced. "I started buying them from the store in Lyons after Sid died."

There was a brief knock, and the door opened. Branson stuck his head in. "We need to wrap this up, folks."

"Give us a few more minutes." I met Branson's gaze and softened my tone. "Please."

He nodded. "Just a few more minutes." Then he pulled back out and shut the door. He didn't even smirk. Impressive.

I refocused on Barry. "Cut to the chase. If it's not illegal to use marijuana here, then you're not in trouble for it. What's the catch?"

He turned to Mom, his tone and expression channeling a wounded dog. "A couple of months ago, right after Sid died, Opal threatened to tell you I was one of her customers if I didn't agree to sell the shop to her." He shrugged pathetically. "I wrote her and told her that I wouldn't be threatened or blackmailed, that there was even less chance I'd sell the property to her now, and I would be taking my business elsewhere."

Mom looked at him expectantly, like there was more to come. But I saw where this was going. "You wrote Opal a note? You actually put it in writing?"

He nodded.

It took substantial effort not to roll my eyes. "So the police have a note from you to Opal, one which announces she was attempting to blackmail you and that you weren't having it. It also confirms you were at least partially involved in her illegal business." One part of this didn't make sense, though I was learning things about Barry that I hadn't expected, so who knew? "So you were aware she was using the kitchen in Heads and Tails? It makes you a part of it. At least I'm assuming she was making her edibles there. Did you know about the marijuana plants growing in the basement?"

The disgust that crossed his face left no doubt

about his sincerity. "No, I most definitely did not. I have no idea how she's had access to the store. I assumed she was making edibles in her bakery with the rest of the candy. And I'd forgotten the store even had a basement. Though if I recall it right, it was nothing more than a crawlspace, not actually a basement."

Thank goodness for that, at least. Though I wasn't sure if his awareness could be proven one way or another. Even if they couldn't get Barry on murder charges, his property was being used as a grow house and distribution center. "Is there any other connection you can think of that would tie you to Opal? Anything at all?"

He considered for a few seconds and then shook his head. "No. I really don't think so."

I believed him.

Barry turned to Mom. "Phyllis, I'm so, so sorry. I swear it's the only secret I've been keeping from you. You know I'm nothing more than an old mountain hippie. Some habits are hard to break." Tears rimmed his eyes once more. "Even for the love of your life."

Tears slid down Mom's cheeks, but she straightened and squared her jaw. "This is a discussion for another time. We'll figure it out." She sniffed. "Are you going to be okay here tonight?"

"I'm not worried about that. I'm sure I'll be fine." Barry glanced over at me. "Will you and Watson stay with your mom tonight? I don't want her to be alone."

"Of course we will."

As if he'd been listening in, another knock sounded on the door and Branson stepped inside. "I'm sorry, but I really do need to end this now."

"Thank you. We're done here." I smiled at him, genuinely grateful for this small gift. And if I put myself in his shoes, or put my father in his shoes, I didn't blame Branson for what he was doing. "We'll call in the morning to see when we can pick him up."

He hesitated. "Well, that will depend on what we might find—"

"You won't find anything else." I intentionally hardened my gaze at him. "And as far as a murderer, you're wasting your time. Eating a magic brownie before bed and killing someone with a rolling pin are very different things. And again, anyone who's met Barry for more than a minute, knows that the second one would never be possible."

Surprisingly, he allowed me to have the last word and nodded as he stepped aside, holding the door open for us.

I stood, then leaned down to kiss Barry on the

cheek. "See you tomorrow." I waited for Barry and Mom to say their goodbyes, then took her hand, and led her out of the police station, intentionally not looking back over my shoulder at Branson.

Just as we walked outside, Gerald rushed toward us. For such a short, round man, he was able to move pretty quickly. I opted to let Mom speak to him while I warmed up the car, otherwise, there might be another murder on our hands.

When we finally pulled out of the police parking lot, Mom finally broke once more, tears streaming, and her frail hands trembling. "I know it's stupid to say, but I wish your father was here. He'd know what to do. You and I both know that if they can find an easy target to pin this on, they will. You don't get much more of an easy target than Barry."

She was right about that. About everything. I took one of my hands off the steering wheel, and clasped hers once again. "I'm not going to let that happen. I promise."

When Watson and I had driven into town that first evening, I'd taken a wrong turn and entered Estes Park a different way than the usual route. Normally we drove up the Big Thompson Canyon, all the while marveling at the massive stone walls that left a person feeling rather insignificant. Instead we'd entered off Highway Seven, which twisted and turned through the forested mountains and then suddenly opened to such a spectacular view I had to pull the car over and get out.

From high above, safely nestled in the valley of several different mountains was Estes Park. I could see the entire little village. The highway continued down, cut through a huge lake, and then into the heart of Estes Park, the quaint little shops and restaurants the center of it all. Houses and neighborhoods spread out from there to the base of the surrounding mountains. The sky had acted as a huge dome, silvery clouds offering a thick blanket of protection over the town. Snow had been softly falling, and the rays of the dying sun cut through here and there, causing bright patches on the earth below. It looked like Watson and I were entering a magical little world contained in a snow globe. It had been such a good omen to the start of my new life. Of the hope I was pinning on this little town and on the Cozy Corgi.

Now as I stood on the sidewalk looking down the rows of shops, wondering where in the world to begin, I could almost picture myself standing on that outcropping of rock once more. Had it really only been two days ago? Things inside the snow globe weren't exactly how I'd envisioned. Far from it. I'd left behind my life in Kansas City after multiple betrayals. I never would have dreamed I was trading betrayal for murder.

Even with murder and some of the stores closed for the winter season, I couldn't deny the town's charm. It was a storybook. The countless shops that filled several blocks of Elkhorn Avenue were a mix of styles, from mountain chalet to log cabin facade and retro fifties and sixties structures. Maybe retro wasn't the right term, since these hadn't been designed to resemble that time period. They'd simply endured over the past six decades. Vintage... that was better than retro any day.

I'd hoped to wake up to find that Mom and I could go down to the station and pick up Barry. No such luck. They were only halfway into their twenty-four-hour cutoff mark, and for some reason, they were going to use Barry as an example. Probably not a fair thought. Branson didn't seem the type for unnecessary power plays. But what did I know? Although, he had me thinking of him as Branson instead of Sergeant Wexler. That in and of itself was a troubling development.

Mom had opened her collection of wires, strings, beads, and healing crystals. I knew she could get lost in her jewelry making for hours. I couldn't sit still. Nor did I have any desire to get my cabin arranged. My brain might've grown comfortable enough to be on a first-name basis with Branson, but it didn't mean I trusted him to keep from pinning all of this on Barry if he could. I wouldn't sit by and watch that happen.

True, maybe I didn't know what I was doing, but I wasn't entirely clueless either. My father had been a detective, my ex-husband a police officer, and my best friend and I had built a multimillion-dollar publishing house solely focused on mystery novels. I could do this.

I pushed aside the tiny voice that whispered I hadn't seen the signs of my husband's affair nor had I realized all those years later that my best friend was getting ready to shove me out of our business. I couldn't dwell on those things, or I wouldn't have a chance of being a lick of help to Barry.

At the end of the day, it didn't matter if I knew how to do this or even if I could do it. I simply had to.

But where to start? I wasn't sure why, but I felt like the answer was somewhere in one of the shops. Maybe simply because downtown was where Opal had been murdered, but anyway, it seemed as good a place as any. That didn't narrow it down too much. Which shop screamed, "We sell clues about murder"? The shop with knitting supplies, the taffy pulling store, the bread bakery, the T-shirt seller, the magic shop that sat right behind the large wooden water-wheel? I discarded the last notion quickly. At least not yet. Officer Green's brother. I couldn't handle any more hostility, at least not so early in the morning. I stared at the waterwheel, though. The river that cut through town was frozen, so the wheel wasn't turning. I knew the feeling. My wheels weren't turning either.

I glanced down at Watson. "I need you to take over, buddy. I'm making emotional connections with the waterwheel. I can't be trusted." I gestured with his leash down the street. "Lead on."

Watson twitched his ears, sniffed the air, then headed out. I was relieved when he passed the magic shop. It would've been just my luck for it to be his first choice. We passed store after store, not pausing at the Native American jewelry shop, the toy store, or scrapbook supply. To my surprise, Watson only wedged his nose under the doorframe of the deli-catessen and gave a great sniff before moving on. The same was true with the cheese shop.

Though the sky was bright, it was cloudy, and the day was cold. It lacked the biting humidity that made the winter in Missouri so much worse, but I still pulled my jacket a little tighter around me. "It doesn't have to be the perfect place, Watson. We just have to start somewhere. Somewhere warm."

He didn't bother looking back and kept right on trotting down the sidewalk. A couple of tourists paused and started to reach out to pet him, but Watson angled away and avoided their outstretched fingers.

I gave an apologetic smile. "Sorry, he's grumpy before coffee in the morning."

They laughed good-naturedly, then ducked into a dress shop.

Coffee! No wonder my brain was foggy. I'd been so antsy to get going I hadn't even taken the time to make a pot. There was a coffee shop a little farther down. We'd stop there.

We were three shops away from caffeine salvation when Watson paused, lifted his nose in the air, then backtracked a few paces and stood in front of a door. I glanced up at the sign, *Cabin and Hearth*.

"Here? Really?" I pointed the way we'd been headed. "We almost made it to coffee."

Watson blinked.

So be it, I was the moron who told my dog to lead the way. The least I could do was actually listen to him when he played his part. "Fine. Have it your way." I pulled open the door, allowing Watson to walk in, and then I followed. The scent of spiced cider wafted over me, instantly making me feel warmer.

A quick glance around threw me off for a second. I'd stepped inside of someone's home. Someone's expensive home. The sensation passed quickly, as the layout wasn't quite right. A large canopy bed made of massive logs sat next to a driftwood bench upholstered in fawn-colored leather. Lamps made of artfully aged metal had cutouts of elk and wolves and glowed amber through their stained glass shades.

There was a commotion somewhere in the back, and a short round woman with cotton-candy, white hair and wearing a gingham dress popped out from behind a display of river rocks that had been painted to look like cats. "Hi there, dear! I thought I heard someone come in." Her eyes widened as she took in my height and then warmed at the sight of Watson. "Well, aren't you just the cutest little thing?" She sank to her knees and held out both hands toward Watson. He barely hesitated before accepting her affection.

Strange.

"Carl! Get one of the dog bones," she called out over her shoulder and then refocused on Watson. "And hurry quick. You've simply got to meet this one!"

Dog bones. Of course. How he did it, I had no idea. Though he was smarter than me, obviously. I should've realized he wasn't looking for clues, just a snack.

The woman seemed to remember I was there, looking up at me again once more. "I should've asked; is it okay if he has a doggy bone?"

"Yes. It is. Thank you." I motioned toward a hall

tree made from nothing but antlers. "Your store has quite... unusual things."

"We try. Many of our items are one of a kind. Just because Estes Park has countless houses and cabins doesn't mean they should all be decorated the same." She gave Watson another quick rub, then placed her hands on her knees so she could stand. "You must be visiting. I'm certain I would've remembered this little guy. What's his name?"

"This is Watson." I held out my hand. "I'm Fred."

"Oh goodness, I'm so bad about that. I'm so sorry. I should have introduced myself. I see a dog and just get all wrapped up." She quickly shook my hand. "I'm Anna. And welcome to town. How long are you visiting? Where are you from?" She rattled off the questions without any real interest. She probably asked them a billion times a day to every customer who walked through the door.

That might be me soon enough.

"I actually just moved to town. Into one of those cabins you're speaking of."

Her blue eyes brightened with interest. "How wonderful! Cabin and Hearth can be your one-stop shop. If you have something in mind you don't see in our store, we can order it or have it custom-made for you."

Just then a man carrying a dog bone emerged from the back of the store. He was short and wide, nearly the exact same build as Anna. The hair lacking on the top of his head was compensated for by his fuzzy white beard. Between the smell of cider and the cute chubby couple, I felt like I was meeting Mr. and Mrs. Claus.

Anna snatched the dog bone out of his hand and waved it around as she spoke, causing Watson's head to whip back and forth. "Carl, this is...." Her eyes narrowed in a look I knew too well. "*Fred*, you said?"

I nodded.

She shrugged and kept going. "She just moved into town. Has a little cabin and is looking for a.... What are you looking for, dear?"

"Sorry to say, I'm not looking for anything at the moment. All of my things are being shipped from back home. I'll have to get rid of things the way it is. Downsizing and all."

Both of their faces fell.

"But I love your store. I'm sure once I get everything arranged, there'll be something I'm missing. From looking around, it looks like there's an entire log cabin lifestyle I wasn't aware of."

"That's true." Anna only looked partially satiated. "You might want to reconsider having your things delivered. I always say, when starting a new life, there's no reason to bring all the things from your old one with you."

I couldn't help but laugh. "You know, my mother was telling me something similar just last night."

Another sweep across the room with the doggy bone. "Sounds like a smart woman. Bring her in, I'm sure she'll help you figure out what you need."

Watson whined.

"Oh, look at me. I'm so sorry, sweetie!" She bent slightly and offered a familiar-looking dog bone to Watson. "These are made locally, right across the street at Healthy Delights. Goodness knows, you won't find much else good there, but dogs definitely love Lois's baking, poor dear."

"Anna!" Carl spoke for the first time. Squeaked, rather. "What a thing to say!" He gave me an exasperated look, and though his tone softened, he still sounded rather like a mouse. "Lois is a lovely lady. And if you're looking for healthy alternatives to sweets, that is exactly the place to go." He patted his belly. "The missus and I obviously aren't prone to such sacrifices."

It looked like Anna was going to argue, so I

jumped in. Plus, it seemed like the perfect segue. "This will actually be Watson's second bone from Lois. And you're right, he loves them." I pointed to the window. "I'm getting ready to open a little book-shop where Heads and Tails used to be. I met Lois when I arrived in town a couple of days ago."

"You?" Like I predicted, it was all the encouragement Anna needed. She let out a gasp and clutched her hands over her breasts. "I heard someone was moving into that shop." Her eyes widened once more, and her tone grew scandalized. "And what a way for you to enter town. I heard you found Opal, not to mention that drug den growing in the basement."

I'd pegged Anna as loving a good story, but I hadn't thought she'd be aware of all those details already. Maybe the stereotype of living in a small town wasn't all hype.

Before I could think of what to say, Anna grasped my hand. "Tell me all about it. I heard she was hit on the head with one of those meat tenderiz-ers. Gladys told me that yesterday. But *I* told *her* it didn't make any sense. What use would a candy maker have for a meat tenderizer?" I marveled at Anna's apparent ability to not need a breath. "I mean maybe she used it to pound nuts or something, but that doesn't seem very efficient for operating the business. Not that I would put much stock in anything Opal Garble does. Or *did*, God rest her soul. The murderous tramp."

"Anna!" Carl's squeak caused Watson to let out another whine, despite still chewing on the dog bone. "The woman was murdered. Don't say such things!"

Anna's tirade had been so frenzied, I barely had a chance to take it all in, and before I could consider what to say, she launched in yet again.

"Don't you get me started, Carl Hanson. Just because the woman is dead, doesn't mean she was a saint." She pointed a ring-encrusted finger in my direction, as if I'd been about to take her husband's side. "Believe me, she had it coming for a long, long time. Why, to tell you the truth, I can't believe it didn't happen years and years ago."

Carl *tsked* and cast an irritated glance at Anna, then refocused on me. "Please excuse my wife. It's a small town, and there's not a lot to do here. Sometimes she can get a little caught up in the rumors floating around about people."

Anna planted both fists on her hips and glared. "Don't you dare act innocent. Wasn't it you, just last night, telling me about Peter Miller—" She glanced my way interjecting with a mock whisper, "He owns a glassblowing shop in between downtown and the national park, and is a happily married man and father of three." Then she turned back to her husband and continued at full volume. "—and how you caught him sneaking around with Gentry Sawyer?" She paused to suck in a quick breath and offered another stage whisper my way. "Gentry owns the Christmas shop, which is close to the glass-blowing place. He is *also* a happily married man and a father of one. He also has a very cute beagle named Snoopy. Not very original as far as beagle names go, if you ask me, but adorable nonetheless." Then back to full volume and addressing Carl. "So don't you talk about me being the one to get caught up in rumors. Not when you're the one making them." With the last few words, she tapped against her husband's chest.

At the look of scandal across his face, and Anna's heavy breathing, it was all I could do to keep from laughing. I decided to milk it and play along. Swiping a page out of Anna Hanson's playbook, I took a step toward them and lowered my voice. "Since you brought it up, I must admit, I did meet Opal the other day as well. She struck me as rather... abrasive."

"Abrasive?" Proving everything his wife just said

was true, Carl's soft-spoken voice lilted and slipped into hyperdrive as he did a complete one-eighty. "I'd say that's a gracious word for Opal." Anna nodded along. "The woman was evil. Pure evil. And a murderer." Unlike his wife, Carl didn't bother with pretending to whisper for effect. "She was known as the black widow around here. She's been married three times."

"*Three* times!" Anna bugged her eyes out. "Three. What kind of respectable woman gets married three times, I ask you?"

"As if that's the point, Anna." Carl cast her an annoyed glance for her interruption. Then back to me. "All three of those husbands? Dead! Every single one. A heart attack here, a car crash there. Black widow, I'm telling you."

"Like I said. Opal Garble had it coming." Anna crossed her arms and lifted her chin.

With his frenzy spent, Carl looked suddenly remorseful. "Well, I still say it's a step too far. One shouldn't speak such things about the dead." He stretched out pudgy fingers and lightly touched my hand that gripped Watson's leash. "What else did you notice when you met Opal the other day?"

I needed to figure out a way to inquire about what happened without becoming known as a town gossip. Although with these two, I doubt it mattered what I said. They'd probably tell any story they wanted about me. So I decided to go for it. "Not much. Just that she was rather rude to Katie, the girl who works for her, and a little dismissive of Lois. Not sure if that's the right word for it. Though I've heard she was the one supporting Lois, so I suppose it makes her not all bad."

They both nodded, but this time it was Anna who spoke. "I have to agree. It was her one redeeming quality. Lois is such a sweet, gentle lamb. Again, her candy making is only fit for... well...." She cast a glance down at Watson. "But even so, Lois deserved a kinder sister. I'd say Opal knew Lois was the one good thing in her life. And the only one who would love her despite her horrid personality. But yes, she was good to Lois, even if it was self-serving."

A gust of cool air swept through the store as the front door opened and a family entered.

Though she looked irritated at being interrupted, Anna raised her voice, sounding cheerful once more. "Welcome to Cabin and Hearth. We'll be right with you. Feel free to look around." When she turned back to me, her smile remained. "Sorry to cut this short, Fred." She bent to pat Watson on the head, but he backed away, his ulterior motive now achieved.

"Well, anyway. Welcome to town. It's good to know someone will be taking over the taxidermy shop. Wait, no, you said you're opening a bookshop, didn't you? That's a much better choice. Just remember, we're right across the street. We'll keep an eye out for you. Just let us know if there's anything at all you need. And bring your mother in. We'd love to help you get your cabin in tip-top shape." She looked over at Carl as if suddenly remembering he was there. "Good grief, what are you still hanging around for? We just got that new shipment of decorative pillows in the back. They're not going to unbox themselves."

Carl gave me a little nod, his gaze not meeting mine, before he walked away.

"Nice to meet you again, dear. I hope you and Watson will be very happy in our little town." Anna offered another smile and a little wave before she headed toward the family.

As we stepped back out onto the sidewalk, the day had grown brighter but no warmer. "If I didn't need a coffee before, I sure do now." I smiled down at Watson. "And you most definitely earned yourself another treat. Granted, those two need a whole bucket of salt to go along with anything they say, but nice choice, Mr. Watson. Nice choice."

I wouldn't have pegged Opal as a murderer, but

if all three of her husbands had died unexplained deaths, maybe that had led to her being bludgeoned. If nothing else, it was a different angle than the edible business she was running. And about as far away from Barry as I could get.

After a large dirty chai and a cranberry-orange scone, I felt ready to go again. The Black Bear Roaster hadn't had dog treats, but I'd given Watson a couple bites of my scone. He'd more than earned it.

Not only had the time inside the coffee shop given me a chance to warm up, but after replaying some of the conversation I'd had with Anna and Carl, I was feeling hopeful. Maybe I actually could do this. I didn't have any real hope of solving Opal's murder, but I was beginning to feel more confident that I could at least get enough leads to punch holes in Barry being the main suspect.

Rebundled against the cold, Watson and I stepped outside, then hurried across the street and began to walk back up the other side of shops. Finding out about Opal's three dead husbands was unexpected, but it didn't narrow down which shops might offer the best leads. I hadn't seen a casket shop among the bunch. Where did one go to find out who was angry about dead husbands? I turned it over to Watson again. But he didn't stop anywhere, just dipped his head and trudged past countless shops. Until we arrived in front of Heads and Tails. At least that was where I thought we were stopping, figuring that Watson recognized our shop. Instead he came to a pause in front of Healthy Delights.

I glared down at him. "Seriously? A huge dog bone and nearly a fourth of a scone, and this is what you have in mind? Granted, I agree, the scone was a little dry and could have used some more white-chocolate chips, but still."

I glanced in the window. The store was dark, just like Sinful Bites. No sign of Katie or Lois, nor did I hear any commotion from inside my shop either that would lead me to believe the police were still there. But I'd been given strict instructions not to enter until I'd received an all clear.

"Sorry, buddy. Your favorite shop is closed." I motioned forward. "Lead on. Where to next?"

Watson simply blinked up at me, then returned his attention to the door of Healthy Delights.

"Fine." I stepped around him. "I suppose you've done enough this morning. We'll see how I do." I led Watson past a shop that did old-fashioned tintype photography, an ice cream parlor, a shop with nothing but cupcakes, and a pet store. The last one, I had to drag him away from. Doubtlessly, he could smell the dog treats inside.

With none of the shops calling to me, we ended up across the street from the waterwheel. Directly in front of Victorian Antlers. I'd expected to drop in later in the day to say hello, but there was no time like the present. Plus, though not at Anna and Carl's level, Percival and Gary could gossip with the best of them.

We were barely ten feet inside the antique store when there was a squeal, and a tall thin man, wearing a deep-purple fur coat, rushed from behind the counter waving his arms in the air, then wrapped me in a huge hug. "I've been waiting for you to drop by!"

I hugged him back. "Hi, Uncle Percival. It's good to see you, as always."

He pulled away, holding me at arm's length as he inspected. "Hair, gorgeous and flawless, as always. Eye makeup"—he waffled his hand—"better than when I saw you last year, but we need to work on a stronger cat eye. Good lip, though. I'm glad you remember it's all about a dramatic eye and a subtle lip gloss." His gaze traveled down my body, and he grimaced. "Still, Fred? Really? Do you really need another lecture? How you can share my genes and still think a broomstick skirt is ever appropriate, I simply can't understand. I swear even Barry's daughters have a more innate sense of style, and I'm fairly certain that man has tie-dye in his veins." He picked a dog hair off my shoulder, and then a smile broke through, and he patted my cheek affectionately. "But nevertheless, you're family, so I must love you despite your fashion taste." His eyes narrowed. "At least tell me you're not wearing cowboy boots under that monstrosity."

"Fine. I won't tell you."

He let out a howl, and I couldn't keep from chuckling.

"That's a lot of criticism from a man wearing a purple fur coat. What animal in the real world is purple, anyway?"

He gasped. "Darling, it's faux fur. I may live in the mountains, but I'm not a heathen. And the color is boysenberry, not purple." Next to her older brother, my mom seemed the epitome of common sense and restraint. His brown eyes twinkled in affection as he looked at me, and he raised his voice once more. "Gary, baby, get out here! Our prodigal niece has returned to the fold!"

A man the exact same height as Percival lumbered from somewhere in the bowels of the overly packed shop. Though he was the same height, the similarities stopped there. At sixty, Gary was ten years younger, soft-spoken, somehow managed to retain his physique from his pro-football days, and was about as excitable as a possum playing dead. His dark face spread into a handsome smile as he pulled me into an embrace. "Good to see you, sweetness." His deep baritone rumbled through me.

They both said their hellos to Watson, who received them with familiar ease but not much more, and then they turned their attention back on me. Percival grabbed my hand and held on. "I talked to your mother earlier this morning. She told me all that was going on. And she said you were doing your own investigation."

"No." I shook my head. "I'm not investigating. I'm not pretending like I'm Dad or anything. But it's ridiculous that they think Barry had anything to do with it. I figure I might as well find out anything I can if it helps clear his name."

"You always were your daddy's girl." There was such affection in Gary's tone that I couldn't help but smile at him as I tried to hold back the burn behind my eyes. Gary had gotten along with my father like gangbusters whenever they'd visited. Mom and Percival chatting about fashion and food and movies, while Dad, Gary, and I talked sports. I never cared all that much for sports, but knew if I waited long enough, Gary would get Dad to start talking about his open cases, and after a few beers, Dad always said a little more around me than he would've at other times.

I decided to cut through the pleasantries. "What do you guys think about Bran...er... Sergeant Wexler?"

"Branson, huh?" Percival's brows shot up, always too quick for his own good. "I'd say he's a handsome devil."

Gary rolled his eyes, but nodded. "He seems like a good man. We've not had too much interaction with him. He's only been in Estes for the past three or four years. Seems like a fair guy, though." He shrugged. "Unless, of course, he keeps Barry in there much longer. You just have to meet the guy for two seconds to know he's not going to do anybody any harm."

I hesitated for a heartbeat, trying to determine if I was betraying Barry's confidence, but figured it was more important trying to find out any other details which could exonerate him than to keep his secrets.

Even so, I glanced behind me as if there were customers in the store. "Did Mom tell you why they're keeping him?"

Percival and Gary exchanged glances, and then Percival pinched his forefinger and thumb together and held them up to his lips while making an exaggerated sucking sound.

It was my turn to roll my eyes. "Yes. Something like that."

"I do hate how your mother found out like she did. She's a gracious woman, but she's never been the most open-minded about substances. Of course being married to your father didn't help the situation, I suppose. I always worried what she would think if she found out about Barry."

"You knew already?" It wasn't like Percival and my mother to keep secrets from each other.

My uncles exchanged glances once more. "Darling, it wasn't exactly a well-kept secret that Opal could get a guy what he needed, at least for those of us who needed it. Granted, we didn't know where she was making them, not that it would've mattered."

"Or that she had a small fortune of pot growing in the basement." Gary let out a low whistle.

I nearly asked if there had been confirmation on the amount of marijuana she'd been growing, but then realized the implication of their words. "Wait a minute. You guys too?"

Gary had the decency to look a little embarrassed. "It's legal now."

Percival let out a snort. "Oh yes, we waited until it was legal." He squeezed my hand before letting it go. "Darling Fred, not everyone grew up in a police state household. Some of us were children of the sixties and seventies. And trust me, edibles barely register. Yesterday's pot is today's kale. Now, if you really wanna have a good time—"

I held up my hand. "Unless you think this can help Barry, please, spare me the details."

"Exactly." Gary glared at his husband for a second, then looked back at me. "Besides, Barry quit going to Opal quite a while ago. True, at the time we didn't know it was because Opal was threatening to spill the beans to Phyllis. Barry just told us he liked the product in Lyons better."

Percival waved him off. "So fill us in. What have you discovered so far?"

"Not much. In fact, outside of stopping for coffee, the only place I've been is Cabin and Hearth."

Gary let out an uncharacteristically loud whoop

and slapped his knee. "You started with Anna and Carl? Girl, you hit the ground running!"

Percival rubbed his hands together in anticipation. "Chances are whatever they said was a bunch of hogwash, but I'm sure it was delicious. What did they tell you?"

Again I hesitated, feeling like if I really was going to look for clues, I needed to keep things to myself. But they were family, and who knew, maybe what I'd heard would trigger something one of them knew but hadn't thought was important. "Well, have either of you heard the rumors of Opal being a black widow?"

"Black widow?" Percival's face fell. "That's all you got out of the Hansons? Sweetie I could've told you that. Everybody talks about her being responsible for killing all those men. Of course nobody's offered a shred of proof. Lord knows, she was mean enough to do it."

"Nah." Gary grimaced. "She wasn't the nicest woman around, but she wasn't a murderer. And I always got the impression she loved every one of her husbands. At least as much as Opal could love anyone outside of Lois. She wasn't a killer."

I glanced at Percival for confirmation. He

shrugged as if the admission cost him. "Yeah. I have to say I agree."

Like in the cabin furniture store, we were interrupted by a gust of cold air, and the four of us looked over at the tiny woman who entered the shop.

I did a double take when I recognized Lois Garble underneath the black veil of her hat. It took her longer to recognize me, but when she did, she halted for a heartbeat and then hurried toward me. "Oh, Fred." She shocked me by throwing her arms around me, at least as far as she could reach. "I was planning on trying to find you today. You were so sweet to me when I was such a mess yesterday. It was the worst moment of my life, but I'm so glad I had you and Katie there to hold me together."

I patted her back and glanced at my uncles, wanting salvation. She really had been hysterical, but Katie had been the one to hold and soothe her. I'd been utterly clueless on what to do and only mumbled some nonsense as I patted her shoulder.

After a second, Lois pulled back and noticed Watson. "Oh, and you, sweet baby. I don't have any of my bones with me. I'm so sorry." She rifled through the basket in her hands, then pulled out what looked like a gingerbread man and looked at me. "Not exactly a dog treat, but it's all natural. No chocolate or anything. Do you mind?"

Watson left out a chuff which clearly meant I'd better not screw this up for him. "Of course. That's very kind of you, Lois."

She handed him the cookie, and Watson took it, then began to prance away. He glared back at the end of his leash. I dropped it so he could wander behind the counter and eat his treasure in peace. Lois pushed the basket toward Percival and Gary. "I've been baking up a storm. That's how I cope. If I stop for even a second, I just end up sobbing. But now I don't know what to do with all the things I've made. I can't bring myself to open the store. I just don't have it in me. Even the thought of going by the shops makes me want to die. It just makes me want to die."

Percival slid the basket of baked goods on the counter with a distasteful look on his face before he and Gary gathered around Lois, comforting her like the wounded little bird she was. "You're not alone in this, Lois. You've got the whole town behind you."

"Percival's right, sweetie. We're all your family now. All of us."

"You are both wonderful." She sniffed, and through the veil, a tear glinted on her cheek. Lois turned to me. "I'm so sorry, how rude. You were here, and I just walked in and interrupted. Please don't let me keep you if you're shopping or need help. I know you have a new house to furnish. I'm sure you need some beautiful antiques. You couldn't find better than Percival and Gary here."

"Oh no, Lois, you're not interrupting at all." Despite myself, I was tempted to pat her on the shoulder again. Lord knew what good that would do.

"Fred is our niece. Her mom is Percival's sister." Gary's smooth voice somehow made such an innocuous statement sound comforting. A skill I most definitely didn't have.

It took her a second, but then Lois let out a little chirp. "Well, that shows you what a mess I'm in. Of course she is. We talked about that when we met the other night. You're Phyllis and Barry's daughter." Another chirp and she left the embrace of my uncles and grabbed both of my hands in hers. "Oh, Fred. I wasn't even thinking." She sniffed. "I heard about poor Barry. Of course I called them instantly and let them know they had the wrong person. Barry's the sweetest man. There's no way he would ever do anything like that to Opal."

I'd already liked Lois, but she stole my heart in

that moment. "You did? You called the police station?"

"Well, of course I did. I want justice for Opal, but not at the price of an innocent man."

"Thank you." It was all I could say before my throat constricted.

She squeezed my fingers before letting go, looking back at my uncles. "And actually, I have to thank you for receiving me so kindly. I've taken a couple of baskets to a few of the other proprietors downtown. Not everyone has been so welcoming. It's so embarrassing I almost just went home. But I can't stand to be by myself right now."

Gary's muscular chest puffed up. "Who's not been welcoming to you, Lois? I can't even imagine."

Lois sighed, the noise making her sound sickly. "I can. I understand it completely. I've never been so embarrassed in my life." She sniffed again. "One minute I'm a sobbing wreck because I don't know how to get through a moment without my sister, and the next I'm just so mad I'm shaking. So humiliating. To find out that some people knew. This whole time, they've probably been looking at me, thinking I knew about what Opal was doing. About the"—she dropped her voice so it was barely audible—"drugs."

Not having any of Gary's skills at comfort either,

Percival nearly squawked. "What! You mean you didn't know?"

Lois started to cry.

I stood several paces away while Gary and Percival tried to put Lois back together again. Right when it sounded like her breathing was becoming close to normal, my cell vibrated in my pocket. It was Mom. I hit Accept and held it to my ear. "Are you okay?"

"Yes!" Her voice was a million times brighter than when I left her that morning. "They just called. They're releasing Barry on bail. But I'm too worked up to drive. Will you please come get me, Fred? We can pick him up together."

NINE

"Those cots at the jail are surprisingly comfortable. The food left a lot to be desired, but it was a great night's sleep." Barry grinned happily at me in the reflection of the rearview mirror.

He and Mom wanted to sit together, so they were crammed into the back of my Mini Cooper. Watson had his typical place beside me in the passenger seat. I'd expected to pick up a frazzled, haggard-looking Barry. Instead, he was chipper, obviously well rested, and bright-eyed.

"Oh, and you'll never guess who my cellmate was last night." Barry clapped his hands together once. "But try. Guess."

Mom giggled and seemed to give it some actual thought. "The first person I can picture in jail would be Mark Green, but I don't think you'd seem so pleased by it if it was him."

He shuddered. "Dear Lord no. I would've had to sleep with one eye open."

I glanced at the rearview once more. "Who's Mark Green?"

"He owns the magic shop." Mom's tone took on an apologetic tone. "I know it's ungracious of me to say, but he's not the nicest of men."

Green. Of course. I should've realized. Officer Green's brother. It seemed the dislike went both ways.

Before I could ask for more details on that, Barry nudged my shoulder from the back seat. "Your turn, Fred. Take a guess."

"Seriously, Barry? You just got out of jail and are playing guessing games?"

He *humphed*. "Fine. I'll just tell you." He turned his attention to Mom, since she was actually interested. "Simon Faulk."

"Who...?" Before Barry had a chance to reply, Mom sucked in a surprised breath. "Oh, Simon! The new manager of Day of Lace. I've only met him a couple of times. But he seemed like a nice young man."

"Very! I was charmed by him. I must say, it was a pleasant way to spend the evening. It seemed he and Rion got into it about a new shipment of wedding dresses, and Simon punched him. Which, honestly, I can't see him doing. He really is a gentle soul." Barry let out a long-suffering sigh. "He got out before me this morning. I must say, the few hours after he left simply dragged by. I never would've guessed there was so much behind-the-scenes drama in the wedding dress business."

Mom made a knowing *cluck*. "Capitalism, dear. Not good for the soul."

I couldn't hold back my laughter, and dared to glance into the back seat. "You do realize you two own at least a fourth of the properties downtown, right?"

Mom furrowed her brows. "I don't see your point, dear."

I knew better than to wade into that murky pool. Though I turned back to the road, I addressed Barry. "And I'm glad you felt like it was a vacation, while Mom and I were worried sick about you last night."

"No need to worry. I have to say, Sergeant Wexler obviously thought I was up to no good, but he was kind with me. I hated he wasn't there when I left. Maybe I'll bring him back a thank-you card or something."

"Don't you dare! I don't care if Opal was trying to blackmail you. And I don't care if Branson was right to hold you on suspicion. We do not give thank-you cards for someone putting us in jail."

"He let me out again, Fred. That counts for something."

I glared at him in the mirror. "Because he was pushing the twenty-four-hour mark, Barry. You're not cleared of anything yet." I loved them both, but sometimes their easy-breezy nature rubbed me the wrong way. "And while we're at it, why didn't you guys fill me in on the rumors about Opal? Maybe this whole thing has nothing to do with her making edibles or growing pot. With three dead husbands, surely there's some angry extended family out there who blame her and want their revenge."

Mom chuckled. "That's just silly, darling. This isn't a Lifetime movie. And those are just rumors. I won't say Opal was my favorite woman in the world, by any means, but she wasn't a killer."

I nearly asked what kind of movies she'd been watching on Lifetime, but decided it was beside the point. "Just because you think so, doesn't mean someone who cared about one of those husbands feels the same. Even if we can't figure out who it is, it's a completely different direction on this case, one that would prove it has absolutely nothing to do with

Barry." I turned off Elkhorn Avenue and onto the road leading to their house.

"Oh, Fred." Mom reached up and squeezed my arm. "Please be careful."

I glanced back at her again, startled. "What do you mean?"

"You just referred to this as a case. You sound just like your father. I'd like to tell you to leave it alone. Let the police handle it. Barry's innocent, it will come through. Whatever's happening, someone killed Opal. And if you're treating this like a case, it means someone's not going to like that you're snooping around." She sighed. "But I also know you are your father's daughter. It wouldn't do any good to ask you to stop, or even beg. So be careful. I can't lose you. I won't."

I didn't know what to say to that. My heart warmed at being compared to my father, which I knew was silly as I was constantly being compared to my father by anyone who knew him, but it still made me feel like he was near every time it happened. I hadn't thought I'd been putting myself in danger. Maybe that was silly too. Asking questions about a murder? Obviously it wouldn't be appreciated by the actual murderer. I ignored that thought as I pulled up in front of their house.

"Maybe you're right. Maybe it has nothing to do with Opal being a black widow. But I'd like you guys to think about those husbands, if you knew them. If they have any family in town. Maybe you might find an option of someone who is capable of killing someone with a rolling pin." After I put the car in Park, I swiveled back to look Barry in the face. "What's the name of your dispensary in Lyons? Or is there just the one?"

He cast a guilty glance toward Mom but answered, "Green Munchies."

Mom rolled her eyes.

Barry refocused on me. "You're going there? I'll come with you."

"Oh, no you don't!" Mom clamped a hand on Barry's thigh. "The last thing we need right now is you being caught buying more edibles."

The insulted expression that crossed Barry's face was nearly funny. "I'm not going there to make a purchase. You just got done telling Fred to be careful. I'm going as backup." He scrunched up his nose and lowered his voice to mutter. "And if I did buy something, it's legal there."

I pointed my finger at them. "Number one, this isn't a case, no matter what I said. Therefore, I don't need backup. I'm just going to check it out and ask questions. Number two, and most importantly"—I gave an unwavering stare at Barry—"you're not going."

"But—"

"You're not going!" Mom and I chimed in unison, and then chuckled at each other.

It began to snow in earnest over the half-hour drive to Lyons. I'd wondered if I'd have to get a new car, considering winter in the mountains. But so far, the front-wheel-drive seemed to be cutting it. I found Green Munchies easily enough. I'd never been in a dispensary before, and had expected to pull up to a dilapidated building that was probably close to being condemned. Instead, the new construction was a modern square of concrete, glass, and lightly colored wood.

During the drive, I convinced myself that my growing nerves were more about the snow and possible slick roads than where I was headed. But the self-deception faded along with my nerves as I looked at the place. It didn't feel like walking into a dangerous drug den at all.

As we weren't in a crowded area, I didn't bother with the leash, letting Watson keep pace beside me as we exited the car and walked up the pristine sidewalk.

I was unable to stop myself from gawking when we entered the store. It was like Whole Foods and Apple had a night of passion and produced a drug-wielding baby. Like the outside, the space was sleek and shiny. The open concept was minimalistic yet had high-end finishes. The cases however, were space-age, massive plastic white ovals which glowed softly. No wonder Barry said things had been more expensive here.

Watson and I slowly passed the first couple of cases. An endless array of what I supposed were pot leaves were labeled with names I would expect at a high-end coffee shop. And on the other side, the baked goods put the stunning display I'd seen in Sinful Bites to shame. I addressed Watson even though I didn't take my gaze from a red-velvet brownie. "Don't even think about getting a snack here. If you keep going as you are, you're going to be so fat you'll be nothing but a ginger-furred log." Not to mention I couldn't imagine how expensive a dog treat in this place would be.

A soft chuckle from behind caused me to jump, and I whirled around. I blinked at the handsome man behind the counter. At least I thought he was handsome, behind the costume. I had to remind myself that Halloween had been a couple of weeks ago.

"Sorry, I didn't mean to startle you." The man smiled gently. "I didn't hear you all come in. Do you often have conversations with your dog?"

Conversations with my dog? I glanced down at Watson, who peered up at me. Huh. I hadn't actually thought of that. "You know, I suppose I do."

"He's a cute little fella. And we do have dog treats here. I know you're worried about him becoming a log, but he would be an adorable log."

Watson yipped at his favorite word.

I ignored him. "No, thank you. He's had enough. And as funny as it might be, I wouldn't consider myself a very good corgi mama if I got Watson high."

Confusion crossed the man's features, and then he shook his head. "Oh no, the dog treats are just boring old dog treats. None of the good stuff in them."

Another yip from Watson.

The man pulled on his handlebar mustache. "Well, even if your dog can't have a treat, we've got lots of treats for you. Any you'd like to check out?"

Watson growled. I glared at him, then cast the

same expression on the man. "You've got to quit saying that word."

More confusion. "What word?"

I pointed at Watson as I mouthed, "*Treat*."

His bloodshot eyes widened, and then he smiled. "Oh. Of course. Sorry." He considered for a moment, pulled on his mustache again. "Well then, any *delicacies* you'd like to try?"

With the second pull of his handlebar mustache, the full picture of his costume came together, and I realized it wasn't a costume at all. The brown fedora with a small red feather, skintight goldenrod-colored shirt under an equally skintight silk vest, gray scarf, and vivid tattoos covering his thin arms, which were revealed by his rolled-up sleeves. He was a hipster. But not like the ones we had back in Kansas City, at least not like any I'd seen. I tried to focus on the task at hand.

I was disconcerted enough being in a dispensary, but the unexpected combination of designer ambience and an updated version of Mark Twain as a drug pusher was throwing me off. "I... er... honestly, I've never been in a store like this before. I'm not really sure where to start."

His eyes glinted. "A virgin. Looks like school is in session." He gestured to different locations around the store. "What do you think you are most inter-ested in? Smoking, vaping, tinctures, oils, edibles?"

Tinctures? "Uhm... edibles?"

"Edibles!" He nodded sagely. "That's what I thought. You look like an edibles type of girl."

Again he took my words away. I looked like an edibles type of girl? I wasn't certain if it was a commentary on my weight or not. And as I was at least fifteen years older than the guy, I wasn't sure he should be calling me girl.

He didn't seem to notice my discomfort, talking to me as he turned and headed across the store to the case with the red-velvet brownie I'd been eyeing. "Edibles are a great place to begin. A lot of people are less nervous around them. You do have to be careful with consumption, though. It's easy to get too much if you don't know what you're doing or if you're not sure of the quality or quantity of mari-juana in the product. I can guarantee you everything we sell here at the Green Munchies is the highest of industry standards, and I'll be able to guide you on the right dosage on whatever you choose." He came to a stop behind the counter, placing both hands on the glass, the lights from the overarching oval casting strange shadows over his features. "The name is Eddie, by the way."

I was still trying to process his spiel, and it took me a moment to land on the appropriate response. "I'm Fred. And this is Watson." I had a moment of panic, wondering if I should have come up with an alias. Too late now, and probably silly to even consider. It wasn't like I was undercover or anything. Or that I was a detective at all, for that matter. I was an ex-professor, turned ex-publisher, turned bookstore owner. That was it.

Eddie pointed at small squares of fudge which had a layer of pecans, swirls of caramel, and crystalline chunks of salt. Mouthwatering. I was going to have to give myself a similar lecture about treats as the one I'd given to Watson.

"These are one of our more popular items. And what I would recommend to someone trying edibles for the first time. It's easy to cut off the amount you need. You can freeze it, and it's just as good later on. That's not always true with some of the baked items." He then pointed to a smooth glistening bar of chocolate. "Of course, this is the same sort of deal, if your tastes run more simply. We also offer a punch card. You get twenty-five percent off a future order once you've spent five hundred dollars. Enrolling is free, and I highly recommend it."

I suddenly felt like I was being pressured to sign

up for Amway or getting a membership to Costco. This was what buying pot was like?

My father was killed before marijuana became legal anywhere in the country. I was certain none of his undercover drug dealings had ever resembled this. I couldn't even fathom what he would say or think if he stepped into Green Munchies, or what he'd make of Eddie.

The thought made me want to bolt. Dad had been on my mind too much over the past day. It made sense, I knew, but it was leaving me shaky. Maybe coming here had been a mistake. At least at the moment. I'd buy something quickly so I'd leave a good impression and get back to Estes. "I'll just get whatever you recommend."

No sooner had the words left my mouth than I could swear I felt my father's disapproval. Or maybe it was just Watson still glowering at me after denying him a treat. Either way, I couldn't waste this moment. But how to turn the conversation without causing suspicion?

The answer was obvious. "My stepdad, Barry, recommended your shop. However, he didn't tell me what he normally gets. Chances are low you remember him or his order." That was a lie. If Eddie had ever been in here when Barry came knocking, I had no doubt he would remember. Although, who knew? Maybe in the dispensary business, characters like Barry were a dime a dozen.

"Barry?" Eddie's voice brightened and lost every ounce of its professional tenor. "Tie-dyed, hippy Barry from Estes Park? That Barry?"

I nodded. Apparently not a dime a dozen.

"Dude! That old guy is dope! Like he's the real thing." Eddie cocked his head, studying me. "Wait a minute, you're his daughter? And you've never tried pot before?"

"*Step*daughter."

"Ahhh." He nodded. "Right. That makes sense, I suppose. Well, I will definitely hook you up. And to top it off, I'll go ahead and give you the twenty-five percent discount today. I love that guy. Meant a lot that even though he could've purchased in Estes, he'd drive all the way down here to the source. A percentage is a percentage, don't get me wrong, but it helps me out when customers come directly to my place." Eddie pulled out what looked like an expensive candy box, and began to fill it with an assortment of brownies, chocolate-covered pretzels, a few cellophane-wrapped hard pieces of candy, and gummy bears. "I assume you want his normal?"

This was his normal? If Barry was buying this

much, I marveled he was able to keep his stash away from Mom. "Sure. That's great."

He continued to fill the box as he spoke. "But seriously, Barry is awesome. Super chill, and like straight-up legit. I swear he taught me a thing or two about how to smoke up."

Good God. If he kept going, I was afraid I was going to learn things about Barry I definitely didn't want to know. Something Eddie said echoed in my mind as he prattled on, and I sucked in a little gasp.

Eddie glanced at me. "You okay?"

I nodded, trying to determine how upfront to be. I decided to go for it. "You said Barry comes to the source? Does that mean Opal got her... supplies from you?"

Eddie jerked, his expression growing dark. Apparently he hadn't realized how much he'd said.

I'd already messed things up. That was fast.

He considered for a moment, then shrugged, though he didn't look any happier. "You're Barry's girl, so you're dope by association." He leaned forward, his voice lowering not so much to whisper but in anger. "Don't get me wrong, I'm a pacifist, but I'm not going to lie. I heard what happened to Opal. I'm not shedding any tears. People like her deserve what they get."

I pressed a little further; why not? "Yeah, Barry seems not to be her biggest fan either. Which, you've met my stepdad. He likes everybody."

"Exactly!" Eddie practically snarled. "Sid and I had a good thing going for years. I'd grow the stuff, give him a fair price, didn't demand too much share of the profit. It was chill. Easy, cordial. Granted, what he did with all those animals wigged me out. I'm a pacifist, like I said." He shuddered but kept going. "Then he started dating that candy woman, and she convinced him they could make a ton more money if they started growing their own product." He straightened, holding his arms out as if he was being crucified. "You know how much I have to pay for the license to grow? How much inspection I have to endure? And she thinks she can just walk in, do it all behind closed doors, and reap all the profit? Like I said, I didn't do her in, but she had it coming."

She had it coming. That seemed the theme around Opal Garble. And she'd been dating Sid? That was news, but I didn't want to let on I hadn't known that part. "She was stealing business from you and getting away with it without having to pay any of the fees and go through all the red tape. Why didn't you turn her in?"

"Believe me, I threatened to. Course that evil

woman just laughed. Told me to go ahead. Said she'd bring me down with her."

"How could she do that? You said yourself you're already paying the fees and going through inspections."

Behind his handlebar mustache, Eddie's cheeks turned bright red. "Yeah, but I was also supplying Sid with product. And Estes Park, with its holier-than-thou attitude, still refuses to let a dispensary inside its town borders." His snarl was back. "As much as I hate to admit it, there was no way I could take Opal down without doing the same thing to myself."

"Ah. I suppose that makes sense." It really did. And it looked like Mom and Barry were probably right. With Opal seeming to be comfortable black-mailing and threatening people, the three dead husbands probably weren't even on the radar. I refocused on Eddie, remembering I needed to play the part of Barry's dope stepdaughter, not that I was really sure what it meant. "Man. That really does suck. Well, at least you know you did things the right way and you don't have to worry about Opal anymore."

"True story." Eddie smiled and relaxed again, another twinkle glowing in his eyes. "Plus, I'm betting another bakery will open to replace whatever shop Opal had. Maybe I'll get my foot in the door once more."

I forced a friendly shrug. "One can hope."

"No doubt!" Eddie held up the box that was nearly filled to running over. "This look all right for you?"

What in the world was I going to do with all of that? "Looks great, thanks!"

"Awesome." Eddie beamed like he'd expected me to say no. "Good thing I'm already giving you a twenty-five percent discount. You're gonna get your money's worth today!" He shut the box and pulled out a green ribbon to tie around it. Definitely not what I expected from a dispensary. "I almost feel sacrilegious for asking this of Barry's stepdaughter, but do you want me to go over how to use this and figure out portion size?"

I shook my head, feeling queasy at the thought. "No, but thank you. I'm sure Barry will make sure I get it all right."

An alarm clock that probably wasn't much younger than me blinked large red numbers from across the dark bedroom. Nearly three in the morning. I was tempted to get up and turn the clock to face the wall so I couldn't see its taunting, but Watson's soft snores drifted up from beside the bed. I didn't want to disturb him.

At least one of us was sleeping.

I kept reminding myself I didn't need to solve Opal's murder. That hadn't been the point. I simply needed to get enough information to cause probable doubt against Barry. Even if it felt like simply meeting Barry once was enough probable doubt in regards to murder. I felt like I already had more than enough. I could take it all to the police, offer it up on a silver platter—or better suited, in the designer box with the green ribbon—and let them have at it.

If it was that simple, I probably wouldn't be

tossing all night, turning over endless possibilities in my mind. What little research Mom and Barry had done on Opal's dead husbands while I'd been at Lyons revealed nothing. At least no more than what everyone else already seemed to know. Three husbands over the span of decades—three *dead* husbands. And while casual gossip held Opal responsible, no genuine allegations had ever been laid at her feet. Plus, the most recent death had been long enough ago that if the husband's families were going to raise a stink, they would have done so before now. Mom and Barry both thought it was a dead end. However, the saying was that revenge is best served cold. Maybe in this case it got served with a rolling pin.

In the dark of night, something about that scenario didn't sit right with me. I couldn't put my finger on why. I simply didn't think her black-widow status had led to her death. After talking to Eddie, I had one more person Opal had either tried to blackmail or threatened. And I'd only been asking questions for a little over a day. My hunch was the list would end up being a long Who's Who of Estes Park. Recreational marijuana use might be legal in Colorado, but it seemed Estes Park was its own entity. Sheltered on all sides by the mountains and

secluded in its own way of life. It was one thing to
threaten a guy like Barry. Mom would be the only
one to be surprised or to care that he partook in
magic brownies from time to time. But what other
secrets were out there? Who else might Opal have
blackmailed? Maybe she had finally crossed the
wrong person.

Watson let out a long whine in his sleep. Probably dreaming of treats. He'd given me the cold
shoulder as we drove back to Estes.

I twisted again and readjusted to curl around one
of the pillows. And maybe it had nothing to do with
threatening or blackmail. Eddie didn't seem any
more capable of murder than Barry, but he was definitely angry. Maybe he'd been a little too emphatic
about being a pacifist. I thought I was fairly good at
reading people, but who knew? I'd never spoken to
anyone with a handlebar mustache before; maybe it
had thrown me off my game. And at *that* gem of a
thought, I realized I was doing myself absolutely no
good. I needed sleep. And I needed to quit trying to
figure out who killed Opal and just be satisfied I had
enough evidence to take the spotlight off Barry.

Though, did I really? I didn't actually have any
evidence. Just gossip and hearsay. Sergeant Wexler
had a physical note from Barry refusing to give in to

Opal's blackmail. I needed something more. Much more.

Watson's whimper brought me out of a dream about chocolate bars with tiny handlebar mustaches waving pot leaves in the air. I glanced at the clock. Not even half past three. I glared down at him. "Really? I literally just fell asleep."

He whined and bounced his front paws.

It took me a second; Watson never interrupted my sleep. Then I remembered where we were. With a groan, I threw back the covers and twisted out of bed. "First thing tomorrow, we're finding a contractor to install the doggy door, and a dog run." I scratched his head. "Come on. It's not your fault."

Watson scampered ahead of me and took his place by the front door, still bouncing and whining pitifully.

I started to open the door, then remembered it was mid-November in the middle of the mountains, and grabbed the coat off the hall tree as I shoved my feet into the snow boots I'd left by the entryway. Watson whined again as I tried to fasten the buttons. Giving up, I reached for the door handle. "Fine. Fine. We don't all have fur coats on, you know." I had barely cracked the door before Watson barreled through.

I was surprised when I joined him outside. Despite the heavy snowfall, there was no wind, the sky was clear, the moon full, and stars illuminated the entire scene. Again I was swept up in the impression of living in a snow globe. I breathed in the crisp pine-scented air and felt myself relax. The move had been the right decision. I just needed to get through this part, help Barry clear his name, and then as soon as the police were done with the store, I could begin setting up my bookshop and building my new life.

Watson trotted over, seemingly content after finishing his business.

"Go ahead and sniff around. I'm not ready to go in yet. But stay close."

He looked at the cabin, then back up at me.

"Oh, good grief. How did I end up with such a finicky, grumpy little man?" I bent down to scratch his ears, but he scuttled away toward the door. Shaking my head, I followed, opened the door once more, and let him inside. I leaned against the wall, suddenly enjoying the view even more framed through the silhouette of the overhang and log columns of my front porch. It was paradise. Though Thanksgiving was still a week or so away, I had the sudden urge to get a Christmas tree. Soon, I could be sitting by the fire, reading a book, while the tree lights twinkled happily in front of the window where snow fell outside. I stuck my hands in my coat pockets and squeezed around me, relishing the notion.

After a tickle on my hand, I withdrew something from my pocket and held it up to catch the moonlight. The feather. I'd forgotten. What a strange thing to have stuffed in my pocket.

The feather! An entirely new option crashed over me, somehow combining with what I'd learned from Eddie earlier in the day. What if none of this had to do with edibles or Opal's attempted blackmails, or her overall unlovable personality? What if it barely had anything to do with Opal herself? She'd been dating Sid.

I twisted the feather again, considering. No doubt the police were taking care of the owl in the freezer, but what if it all centered around that? Weren't owls an endangered species? I was fairly certain I'd heard something like that. Maybe only certain species of owls. Those big black eyes flashed in my memory. There had been a lot of death in Heads and Tails. Opal, Sid himself, countless animals.

Wonderful. Just what I needed. Some other bunny trail.

I stared at the feather a few more minutes, considering, then stuffed it back into my pocket and went inside. By the time I entered the bedroom, Watson was already asleep in his doggy bed beside my four-poster. "You've got it so good, you don't even know."

I tiptoed across the room and slipped into bed, rearranging the pillows and pulling the covers up to my chin.

The red flashing lights mocked me from across the room, reminding me I'd forgotten to turn the clock around.

Watson let out a contented, dream-laden sigh, and I rolled my eyes.

Well, whatever. It wasn't like I was going to get any sleep anyway.

I didn't have internet service at my cabin yet, so I considered going to the library or Mom's to do a little research first thing in the morning. However, I doubted I'd be able to identify what kind of bird the feather belonged to on Google. There had to be countless brown feathers with light spots. I'd noticed a bird shop downtown the day before. It looked like nothing more than endless birdfeeders and seed, but maybe they would know.

Bundled up for the cold, Watson and I hopped in the Mini Cooper and took off. We were halfway to downtown when I realized I was missing the obvious. I lived in Estes Park, which cuddled up next to Rocky Mountain National Park. I had a whole forest full of animal experts at my fingertips.

I took the time to stop by Black Bear Roasters to get a dirty chai and try my luck with a different pastry. Maybe the bear claw would be a little moister. Made sense, since the place had the word *bear* in its name.

No such luck. At least for me. Watson, on the other hand, thought his half was perfection.

We drove through downtown and up the couple of miles of winding road that took us through various neighborhoods until we neared the entrance of the national park. The snow had stopped, and the day was bright. The end result had turned Estes Park and its outlying scenery into a Christmas village. It would've been much more fun to be at home decorating the Christmas tree than trying to solve a murder.

The thought gave me pause.

Well, I supposed I might as well admit it to myself. Mom was right. I wasn't simply trying to clear Barry's name. I wanted to solve the thing. Wanted Dad to look down on me, grin, and whisper, "That's my girl!"

And truth be told, setting up a Christmas tree didn't sound near as fun as solving a murder.

With an odd sense of giddiness, I pulled the car up to one of the tollbooths that looked like tiny log cabins. I rolled down the window and waited for the ranger inside to look my way.

He didn't.

After a second, I decided to knock, and reached forward. The seatbelt held me back. With a growl, I unfastened it and tried again, rapping on the cold glass.

The ranger jumped and gave a sharp holler as he whipped around to look at me.

Though his eyes were wide in surprise and his features relayed shock, I had an out-of-body experience, or at least as close to it as I'd ever come. Oscar De La Hoya stared back at me.

In other words, my dream man stared at me. The only time I really enjoyed the sport conversations Gary and Dad had was when Oscar De La Hoya had one of his boxing matches on the television. I pretended not to notice, but the man was beautiful. And I could never understand how someone with a face like his made his living by getting it hit.

Oscar slid open the window, and his shocked expression turned to a smile as he gave a little laugh. "Sorry about that! I was totally in my own little world there. Glad the window was shut. You probably would've heard me scream like a five-year-old girl."

I think my mouth moved, but I wouldn't swear to it. Whatever it did, it failed to make any words. He was even more beautiful in person than on screen.

His dark eyes narrowed in concern. "Ma'am? Are you alright?"

And that word was a brick to the forehead. A needed one. The man in front of me was Oscar De La Hoya back when I was in seventh grade. This kid was probably twenty-five and saw me as a *ma'am*.

And here I hadn't even bothered with Percival's lessons of a dramatic cat eye and simple lip gloss that morning.

Oscar leaned out the window and touched my arm. "Are you needing assistance, ma'am?"

From up close, I realized that Oscar De La Hoya was more beautifully cute than actually handsome. Attractive, to be sure, but there was more of a boyish quality to his good looks than the dark sultry edge that Branson Wexler seemed to possess in spades.

"Do you need me to call someone? Maybe a doctor?"

"Has anyone ever told you that you look like Oscar De La Hoya?"

Oh my God! Oh. My. God!

My mouth had worked, only, not really.

He flashed a brilliant smile. Why would anyone with a face like that allow someone to come at it with boxing gloves? "Yeah, I get that all the time. Although that guy's pushing fifty, so I'm not exactly sure if it's a compliment or an insult."

"How old are you?" And again with the mouth vomit! Maybe the staggering amount of edibles in that stupid box from that stupid shop had permeated the air while I lay in that stupid bed. I had to be high as a kite; that was the only explanation.

"Thirty-one." His beautiful smile turned playful. "How old are you?"

"Thirty-eight." I said it like I'd just been given a birthday present. He wasn't twenty-five. There was only seven years between us. That wasn't so....

And again—*Oh. My. God.*

I turned to Watson, desperate for him to save me from myself.

He blinked at me.

Traitor. Then I realized I could save myself. I snatched the feather from the cup holder and held it out for Oscar to take. "Is this from an endangered owl species?"

He flinched back, and I realized I'd bumped the feather against his nose. Still smiling, he took the feather and inspected it.

I had the impression that his smile had transitioned from the genuine kind to the type someone used when confronted with a crazy person who they feared might eat their face.

Oscar ran a finger over the edge of the feather, his brows knitted. Finally he looked back at me. "I have no idea."

"You don't?"

He shook his head. "Sorry to disappoint you. Unfortunately we disappoint a lot of tourists. We're always getting feathers, rocks, leaves, sometimes little portions of twigs. While I know the names of more items in the park than your average bear, I'm not actually an encyclopedia."

"Oh." So not only had I just made a complete fool of myself, I'd done it for no good reason.

He chuckled softly. "I gotta say, I've never had someone look so disappointed when I didn't know the answer to something like that. Do you and the feather go way back?"

Probably because I already felt like the biggest fool in the world, I bristled at his teasing and snatched the feather from his fingers. "No. Not all that long. Sorry to have bothered you." I turned to face the road, ready to pound the gas and drive away as quickly as possible. I might just keep on going. After this, it might be a good idea to start a reset on life somewhere else.

"Ma'am." I deflated at his use of that word once more and looked back at Oscar to see him motioning over the top of my car toward a larger cabin a little ways off the road. "I have a computer in there. We can look it up if you really need to know."

"No, thank you. I don't need to waste your time. I'm sure I can do that part on my own. But thank you again. That's very sweet of you, Oscar."

I realized my mistake as his eyes bugged once more and his smile returned. He leaned forward and whispered, "Would you be disappointed if I told you I've never been in a fight in my life, much less in a boxing ring?"

I couldn't help but laugh. "Actually, that makes me feel better. I've never understood why someone with a face as cute as Oscar's would allow himself to be hit."

And once more, the expression on his face let me know that I'd messed up again. "Cute, huh?"

I felt my cheeks burn.

He didn't give me a chance to peel out and drive myself over the edge of a cliff. "I'm Leo Lopez. And your face is too beautiful to let people punch as well."

He rendered me speechless, again. Beautiful?

Leo angled around so he was looking into the passenger seat and addressing Watson. "Would you let your mama know that in polite society it's customary for the other person to share their name as well during an introduction?"

To my surprise, Watson crossed the console and stood with his front paws on my thigh and stretched out to Leo, allowing himself to be petted.

Though they looked nothing alike, it seemed there must be a little bit of Barry Adams in Leo Lopez.

"Um, this is Watson, and his mama who can't seem to string two intelligent words together this morning is Winifred Page. But everybody just calls me Fred."

"A beautiful woman named Fred?" His brown

eyes met mine again, and though there was a teasing glint then, I was surprised to see sincerity as well. "You're definitely the first of your particular species I've ever met." He paused long enough for there to be a spark of heat, unless I was imagining things again, and then motioned over the car once more. "Seems like that feather is pretty important to you. I may not know what it is exactly, but I probably have ways to find out quicker than you. May I save you some time?"

I nodded, not trusting myself to try to use the English language again, and he motioned once more.

"Go ahead and pull in on the side of the road. I'll meet you there."

By the time I parked, Leo was already out of the tollbooth and nearly to the cabin. As I approached him, I realized he was also several inches shorter than Branson, and was almost the exact same height as myself. He seemed a little surprised as well as I approached. I didn't think the glint in his eye dissipated, though.

He held the door open for us. "Just remember, the next time you're in the park, make sure you have a leash on Mr. Watson, here. Not only is it the law in the national forest, it's simply good practice. I'm constantly hearing about coyotes and mountain lions darting out to get people's pets. Just the other day a cougar got the family cat in the backyard during their daughter's birthday party." He shuddered, but chuckled. "That's going to be some expensive therapy later on."

It felt like he poured ice water down my back. I could envision Watson out in the moonlit snow the night before. It hadn't even entered my mind, which, looking back, was beyond stupid. We lived in the mountains now, not the upscale Plaza of Kansas City. I mentally redesigned the dog run I'd been planning for Watson. I didn't care about the cost; that thing was going to be top-of-the-line and as safe as I could possibly make it.

"Sorry. Didn't mean to startle you." Reading my mind, he bent down to pet Watson, who was still acting like he was in love. "No harm done. Your little guy is safe. And it's common for tourists to make that mistake. Like I said, what happened to the cat was someone local who should have known better. Don't feel too bad."

"No, don't be sorry." I forced a smile, though the sense of guilt still bit at me. "I'm glad you mentioned it. I'm not a tourist. I just moved to town. I'm opening a bookstore in the old taxidermy shop. And I've been planning on installing a dog run for

Watson at my house. I wouldn't even have thought...."

"Oh, welcome to town! And don't stress about it. I'll give you the number of one of my friends who does construction. He's more than able to design something for your corgi that will keep him safe. It won't be cheap, but it'll be worth it. In fact—" His expression changed suddenly, and his gaze focused on the feather I held in my hand. "Wait a minute, you're taking over the taxidermy shop? I heard about Opal." He looked up at me and then back at the feather again. "Is that from there?"

I nodded. "Yes, I found it behind a freezer. There was a dead owl inside. But I'm not sure if this feather belongs to that particular bird or another. Or if it even matters."

"Oh, it matters." He plucked the feather out of my hand and crossed the room to sit in front of a computer. "We do the best we can, but poaching is a constant problem. Sometimes worse than others. I've wondered if Sid played a part in that, not that it matters anymore since he passed, but I'd still like to know. I raised my concerns with the police about his shop, but without any evidence, there was nothing they could do."

I took my place over his shoulder and watched as

his fingers flew over the keyboard. He definitely knew where he was going, and images and lists of species flashed across the screen. If I'd been on my own, I would've spent hours trying to decipher all the information, probably to no avail. But within three minutes, Leo clicked on an image and rolled a few inches away to give me more room. "Does this look like the owl you saw?"

The owl was beautiful. Warm dark brown with white spots covering it, causing it to look like it was caught in a snowstorm, with darker striated feathers near the tail. And huge black eyes. I supposed all owls had huge black eyes. "I think so. Granted, you could probably put up a lineup of five different owls and I might not be able to tell the difference, but I think so."

"It's the Mexican Spotted Owl, not endangered but federally threatened." Leo held the feather between us again. "Do you mind if I keep this? I'd like to do a little more research on it. Ask my supervisor."

For some reason I hated to let it go. But I nodded anyway.

"Thanks, I appreciate it. Any help we can get stopping poaching is priceless." Leo laid the feather by the computer, and when he looked back at me, that unnamable twinkle had returned to his eyes. "May I get your number? Just in case the feather is useful? I figure you'd like to know."

I'd come to Estes Park to hit Reset on my life. In every aspect. And one of those aspects was leaving behind a world that was constantly connected to my ex-husband. This new life didn't have room or the desire for a relationship. Or for men in any sort of romantic entanglement. This life was about Fred Page, Watson, and creating my dream bookstore. Simply having a calm and pleasant life. I didn't want anything more complicated than having to search for rare first edition books for persnickety shoppers.

Yet here I was, barely two days into that so-called reset of a life, and I was investigating a murder. Even more terrifying, I found myself giving Leo Lopez— the Oscar De La Hoya of the Rocky Mountain National Park Service—my phone number.

I didn't remember Watson and me walking to the car or driving back out of the national park. The fog lifted on the way to downtown. I stared at Watson in accusation.

"What was that? You were all over the guy like you'd known him for years. Letting him scratch your ears, looking at him like he was Barry's long-lost brother. He didn't even offer to give you a treat!"

Watson's ears perked up at the word, and he turned expectant eyes on me.

"No way, you Benedict Arnold. You only get treats when you stop me from acting like a complete moron and attempting to ruin our new life here. Absolutely no treat for you."

He whimpered and looked longingly at the glove compartment, then back at me, his adorable large brown eyes full of pleading.

"Oh, fine!" Steadying the steering wheel with my left hand, I punched the button for the glove compartment, treats and paperwork spilling out everywhere. Watson had a heyday.

ELEVEN

Watson and I drove back to downtown. If I'd been thinking clearly, I probably would've gone home and taken time to write down my thoughts and things I'd discovered so far, minimal though they were. It would've given me a chance to process through new possibilities and come up with a game plan. However, that would have required clear thinking. The combination of discovering the feather might belong to a threatened owl species, which pointed away from the edible connection, and Leo's reaction to me made any chance of thinking clearly an impossibility.

Or maybe it was *my* reaction to Leo that was throwing me off.

Or maybe it was my reaction to *Branson* that was throwing me off.

I wasn't supposed to be thinking about any man, let alone two. If any clear thinking was happening at all, I would've put a pin into my investigation and found out if there was a nunnery near Estes Park and taken vows of chastity as quickly as possible.

Probably well enough I didn't check. I doubted they let new nuns keep corgis with them in the room. But seriously? I hadn't had a tingle of romantic notions since my divorce six years before. Well, before that, truth be told.

Telling myself it had nothing to do with shoving thoughts of Branson and Leo out of my mind, I hooked the leash to Watson's collar and we strolled the downtown once more. Proving my brain hadn't turned into complete cotton candy, my first stop was to Wings of the Rockies, a store specializing in wild birdseed, feeders, and so much ornithological para-phernalia the place felt a little like a cult headquar-ters. With one mention of the Mexican Spotted Owl, the owner demonstrated her ability to sound like an Animal Planet documentary. But ultimately she offered nothing useful to anyone who wasn't covered in feathers.

We paused to grab a burger and fries from Penelope's for lunch, before checking out the pet shop. I didn't have much hope that a pet store would offer anything helpful with any aspect of my leads, and I was proven correct. But the owner,

Paulie Mertz, a peculiar little man, owned two corgis of his own. Flotsam and Jetsam. It seemed he was also an avid Little Mermaid fan. Before I managed to leave the store, I'd inexplicably allowed myself into promising a corgi playdate a week from Friday.

As we walked out the door, I crashed into someone and accidentally stepped on Watson's paw as I attempted to backpedal. He let out a shrill yip and I shuffled to give him space, once more bumping into the person.

"I'm so, so sorry. I was rushing and I—" My words dried up as I looked into cold blue eyes.

Officer Green glared at me, her hatred clear. She was in her street clothes, a surprisingly feminine sweater and skirt. She looked different enough that if it weren't for her eyes, and her revulsion, I might not have recognized her. "What are you doing, *Fred?*" The amount of disgust she was able to muster at my name was impressive.

"I'm just asking questions to—" I shut my mouth, biting my tongue in the process. I really was thrown off, if I was actually going to answer that question honestly. I had to take a second to remember where I was. Flotsam and Jetsam. Unwanted playdate. Pet shop. "I was asking if there was any way to special order Watson's preferred dog food. They don't carry it here."

Her eyes narrowed as she glanced over my shoulder toward the door, then sneered at me again and gestured toward Watson. "Watch where you're going. And I hope your *dog's* tags are up to date. I'll have to check on that the next time we run into each other." And with that she was gone.

I stared at her as she stormed off. I don't think anyone had ever hated me so much. How could anyone hate a near stranger so deeply? Maybe she'd killed Opal. Just for fun.

Watson and I had barely taken a step away from the pet store when I pictured Officer Green returning to ask if I'd really been checking on special order dog food. With a sense of dread, I turned around and walked back in.

A hundred dollars of special ordered dog food Watson would doubtless refuse to eat later, we ended by walking a block or so away from the main strip to the Christmas shop and the glassblowers. Likewise, I didn't truly expect any connection to Barry, but given that the owners had come up in Anna and Carl's gossipfest, I figured I should at least drop by. Neither owner was in.

By three in the afternoon, Watson and I had

nothing to show for our efforts besides getting to know more of the townspeople and possibly burning off a third of the calories from the burger I'd devoured at lunch. Feeling like a complete failure and that I'd wasted several hours on nothing, I pulled out the number of the contact Leo had given me for Watson's dog run. To my surprise, he agreed to meet me in less than an hour at my home.

Leo hadn't been wrong. I nearly choked when presented with the written estimate for the job. Though, I couldn't argue that the man was thorough. I suppose there might be a chance he was milking a newbie and her love for her dog, but I didn't care. I agreed to burying the dog run a foot and a half into the ground, a reinforced roof, complete with an additional overhang that matched the existing roof on the house to provide shelter, and a triple layer of mesh fencing, that was guaranteed to keep out any predator. To top it all, the construction could start in three days. Watson would be safe, and I could sleep through the night. I decided it was priceless.

Between the hours of unproductive questioning and waving goodbye to thousands and thousands of dollars for Watson, I decided comfort food was in order. Within an hour, I was back from the grocery store, had tomato soup bubbling away in a pot on the stove, and was slathering the bread for grilled cheeses with butter. I'd already stoked the fire and set my Kindle on the arm of the recliner nearby. I needed a night to turn my brain off. No thoughts of men, past or present, no twists and turns of murder or investigations. The only thing that could make it better was having my actual books in the house, and my own overstuffed armchair by the fire. But this would do in a pinch. I'd already decided I was going to reread *Anne of Avonlea*, a childhood favorite. I had enough mystery for the day. It was time for comfort.

A knock sounded on the door just as I placed the grilled cheese on the sizzling pan. I glanced at my cell—no missed calls. Chances were it wasn't Mom or Barry. I didn't want to see anyone. I was officially peopled out.

A second knock, barely ten seconds later.

With a grumble, I removed the grilled cheese and turned off the burner. Someone had driven all the way out to my cabin; they weren't going away easily. And with my Mini Cooper gathering snow outside, I couldn't pretend I wasn't home.

Watson followed me to the door, growling the whole way.

I started to look for the peephole, then realized there wasn't one. That wouldn't do. One more thing to pay for. I nearly threw open the door, then realized how stupid it would be. Especially with everything going on. And while Watson's growl sounded vicious, he wasn't exactly the best guard dog. I paused with my hand on the door handle. "Who's there?"

"Sergeant Wexler. I just need a little moment of your time."

I recognized his voice instantly. It didn't pass my attention he used his formal name and his tone didn't sound overly friendly. So much for not thinking about men that evening. I opened the door, and the breeze ushered in a small gust of snow. I stood aside to make room. "Come in out of the cold."

"Thanks." He stomped his feet on the porch, then stepped in.

Add doormat to the things to purchase.

I shut the door and turned to look at him. Watson growled softly a few more seconds and then let it fade away. Words left me for a moment. It was my first time seeing Branson out of uniform. He made quite the picture in the uniform, don't get me wrong, but Branson in civilian clothes was just as arresting. Flecks of snow glistened in his black hair, and his body seemed impossibly more fit and male under a green flannel shirt, brown leather jacket, tight dark-wash jeans, and snow boots. The stern expression on his handsome face helped cut through my unintentional admiration and helped me find my voice.

"What can I do for you?"

"You can explain why you're harassing the shop owners of downtown, for starters."

I flinched. "Harassing?"

His eyes narrowed. "What would you call it?"

I started to say that I would call it investigating, then realized that probably would sound even worse. I allowed my gaze to travel over his body once more, this time intentionally, and making sure to take any attraction away. "I'm not sure it's any business of yours, *Branson*. It doesn't seem like you're here on official business."

"I came like this as a courtesy, Fred." He glowered, the expression suited his thick brows and angled jaw. As did his low rumble. "However, if you need it to be official, I can happily put on the uniform and call you down to the station." He shrugged. "It's up to you."

Watson growled again, drawing Branson's attention downward.

"Your mom is safe, little man. Don't get your hackles in a bunch." His gaze flicked to mine, though he still addressed Watson. "She'll always be safe with me."

My heart gave a little flutter, and I felt the truth of his words. If he'd been in his uniform, I could've chalked it up to that. I equated the police with safety, with my father. But standing there in his flannel shirt, with his wide shoulders and barrel chest, I couldn't deny my instincts told me I was indeed safe with Branson Wexler. No matter his mood.

My stomach rumbled, and I latched on to it. Maybe there hadn't been a heart flutter after all, just a reminder my dinner was waiting. I considered for half a second, then decided I was tired of overthinking, and motioned back toward the kitchen. "I was just making dinner. Tomato soup and grilled cheese. Want some?"

Those bright green eyes widened in surprise, and some of his apparent irritation dissipated. "I... uhm...." His gaze flicked to the fire, then back at me, and for the second time that day, I saw a spark of heat in a man's eyes.

More as a reaction to myself than Branson, I waved him off and headed back toward the kitchen. "Don't make a deal out of it. I'm hungry. You interrupted dinner. You can either join in or watch me eat as you accuse me of things I've not done."

He chuckled as his footsteps trailed after me. "Grilled cheese and tomato soup sounds perfect. Thank you."

A mix of thrill and *Oh my Lord, Fred, what are you doing?* shot through me. "Great. Do you like mayonnaise on your grilled cheese? Or do you not know how to eat it correctly?"

Another laugh, this one full. "Didn't know you had such a sick sense of humor."

I turned the burner back on and glanced at him. "I wasn't kidding."

He paused as if waiting for a punch line, then gave a slow nod. "Well, all right then. No, thanks for the offer, but I will take my grilled cheese incorrectly, it seems."

"Your loss." I started buttering bread for his grilled cheese. Was I flirting? Surely not. "But don't you dare ask for a bite of mine when you see how much better it looks." Someone shoot me. I was flirting.

"Don't worry. I think I will be fully satisfied." Branson crossed the kitchen, slid out of his jacket, which he hung on the back of a chair, and leaned an elbow on the counter. "Can I help you in any way?"

Despite myself, I did an actual double take, then simply shook my head and refocused on unwrapping the cheese, fearing my reaction would convey too much. Such a small thing. A thing I knew should barely be noticed, let alone cause warmth to spread through my body. It was an offer my father would have given my mother, one that Barry gave her now. But it was an offer Garrett had never given me in our eight years of marriage. "Thanks. The glasses are in the cabinet to the right of the sink. If you'll fill them with ice, that would be great. There are trays in the freezer."

"You got it." And without hesitation, Branson began to fill the glasses. "Cute kitchen. I like the retro style. However...." He chuckled softly. "I know I've only met you a couple of times, but I consider myself a very good reader of people. Not in a million years would I have pegged you the type for choosing tie-dye curtains with—" His eyes narrowed, and he leaned forward slightly. "—flamingos?"

Giving in to the ease I felt with him, I offered a smile. "You'd be right. Those were a welcome-home present from Mom and Barry. At the time, I planned on replacing them as soon as possible, but they're already growing on me."

"Ah, glad my skills aren't fading away. You keeping them because of your family also matches my impression of you."

I couldn't tell whether it was flirtation or not, but I opted to take it as a compliment.

Dinner was ready within a matter of minutes, and we settled in at the small sea-foam green wooden table in the center of the kitchen.

Branson let out a long satisfied groan at his first bite of grilled cheese, which he dipped into the tomato soup. "Boy, does this ever hit the spot. It's been a long day, and I haven't eaten since breakfast."

I held my sandwich midair as I responded. "It'd be better with mayo." Then I took a bite. He was right. It did hit the spot. We ate in silence for a few minutes, some of the ease that had existed while I cooked evaporating. "If I recall, you came here to say not nice things about me. Might as well get that over with."

He sighed, like he'd rather skip the whole thing, but then his expression hardened slightly. "I had reports that you've been going around downtown asking questions to all the shop owners. What's that about?"

He'd had reports? Officer Green flashed through my mind. Yeah, I was willing to bet I knew exactly where those reports had come from. I took another bite of the sandwich, more to give myself a few moments to consider how to best respond. I hadn't done anything illegal. "I'm a shop owner myself now. Don't you think it's a good idea to get to know my fellow business owners?"

He rolled his eyes, though his expression spoke more amusement than irritation. "How about this, Fred. Don't treat me like I'm an idiot, and I'll give you the same courtesy."

I couldn't help but laugh. Nor could I help feeling even more comfortable with him. "Fine. We were just going around, simply asking questions, putting out feelers. Opal was killed in my shop. Right in the heart of downtown Estes Park, surrounded by businesses and people she'd worked with for years and years. It only makes sense that someone, somewhere, might know something."

Branson started to speak, then paused to chew and swallow. "We?"

I gestured toward Watson with my sandwich. "Yes. We."

Watson's ears perked up as Branson looked over at him, probably hoping he was about to get some of the grilled cheese. Branson chuckled again. "Of course. We." He refocused on me, his tone growing a little more serious again. "If it's so innocuous, why did I get a call from Myrtle Bantam squawking about being interrogated about endangered species of owls?"

The fidgety owner of Wings of the Rockies flashed through my mind, and I gave an unladylike snort. "You totally did that on purpose."

"I don't know what you're talking about." The corner of Branson's lips twitched, giving him away.

"Squawking? The owner of the bird store was squawking?"

He shrugged, all innocence. "You met her. Wouldn't you say it's an apt description?"

I would actually, not that I was going to give him the satisfaction. "I'd say it was low-hanging fruit, and you can do better."

He leaned closer to me across the table, his eyes twinkling. "Her last name is Bantam. Did you know that's a type of chicken? I mean, come on. Talk about low-hanging fruit."

I hadn't known that, and I laughed again. "That's pretty wonderful. It's a good thing I'm not a police officer. I'd probably abuse my power and check to see if she'd altered her name."

He leaned closer still. "Oh, I have. And the delicious part? She hasn't changed her name. She truly might be part chicken." He let his gaze linger a few seconds longer, causing my traitorous heart to beat a little faster, and then he leaned back once more. "So back to my question. Why, if you're doing nothing more than meeting your competition, is Myrtle Bantam calling to squawk at me again?" He took a spoonful of soup.

"I didn't say I was meeting my *competition*." Genuine irritation sliced through me, though not at Branson. So it wasn't Officer Green after all. At least not *only* Officer Green. "And I don't know why she's calling to complain. If anyone was harassed, it was me. She... *squawked*... on and on for nearly forty minutes about owls. Believe me, if you've ever wondered about all the interesting things that can be found in owl pellets, I can fill you in. And if you're not sure, an owl pellet is the mess of leftovers the owl vomits up when they're done eating. And again, I'll remind you, it was forty minutes. Forty! About owl vomit. Would you like to take my formal complaint now, or should I come down to the station?"

Branson leaned back in his chair and howled with laughter. When he finally looked back at me, he had to wipe away the tears from his eyes. "Welcome to town, Winifred Page."

I glowered at him and mentally promised myself I would never direct business toward Myrtle Bantam if I could keep from it.

"After her call"—though there was still humor in his tone, his expression grew serious once more—"I checked in with a few other shops. It sounds like you've been busy. I don't think there was one you haven't gone in."

For all the good it did me. "Like I said, I'm getting to know my neighbors. You still haven't listed anything harassment-like."

This time, when Branson's expression shifted, it grew darker. "I also got a rather vexing call from one of the rangers in the national park. He was quite adamant he had proof, after a visit from you, that I'd been lax in taking his unfounded claims seriously." He leveled his stare on me. "You're a smart woman, Fred. I'm fairly certain you realize the national park isn't one of the shops downtown."

Leo had called Branson? Though baseless, something about Myrtle Bantam made it easy to picture her calling to complain; that wasn't true about Leo. "Don't ask me to believe Leo said I was harassing him. I simply had a suspicion I needed some help verifying."

"No, he made no such claims." Branson's eyes narrowed, and though I thought it was at the mention of Leo's name, I couldn't be sure. "But while we're at it, that's one of the other things I wanted to talk to you about. It seems you took evidence from your shop with you the other day. I'd be willing to chalk it up as not realizing the importance of what you had with that feather. Do you make a habit of taking things from crime scenes? I would think the daughter of a policeman would know better."

I stiffened, his words feeling like a slap. "That was a low blow, Sergeant Wexler." My temper spiked. "And no, I don't. I stuffed the feather in my pocket before I found Opal's body. I didn't even think about it again until last night when I felt it in my pocket. And as far as what I'm doing? You've accused my stepfather of murder. And as the daughter of a policeman, I understand why, I understand the steps, and won't hold those against you. However, I also am aware that sometimes *low-hanging fruit* is the easiest thing to grasp at, and that overworked and under-budgeted police stations might see an easy way to close a case." My volume rose, I tried to reel it back in, but to no avail. "And furthermore, judging by what Leo told me, it sounds like I have reason to be concerned. Sid had a federally threatened owl in his deep freezer. Maybe Opal's murder had nothing to do with edibles at all, or with her attempting to blackmail Barry, and doubtless other people. Perhaps it has everything to do with her poacher boyfriend."

Branson's expression shifted several times over my tirade, but his eyes widened in surprise at the last revelation. "Opal was dating Sid?"

"Yes."

He shuddered. "Now that was a visual I never wanted to have in my head."

My irritation didn't allow me to find humor in it. "See, right there. Just by asking questions, I uncovered something you had no idea about."

Branson sighed and offered a small smile, and for the first time, sounded condescending. "A detail which doesn't help your stepfather at all. Sid died months ago. A heart attack, not murder. Opal was killed in the kitchen where she was making edibles. In a building where she was growing a forest of marijuana plants in the basement. A building owned by your stepfather, who we know Opal attempted to blackmail. I can guarantee you Opal wasn't killed because of a *feather*."

"You can't really believe Barry would kill someone." My fingernails dug into the soft flesh of my palms.

"No, I don't." Branson's tone didn't soften. "But despite being good at my job, I've been wrong before.

And because I'm good at my job, your stepfather is still on the suspect list. The very short suspect list."

"Exactly. Good at your job or not, you're making mistakes and not looking in the right direction." I squared my shoulders and lifted my chin. "Someone has to do the legwork. And if I can't trust the police department to do it, then I will."

"Fred." Branson spoke through gritted teeth. "I understand you want to clear Barry's name, and I also understand your father was a detective, so you feel somewhat... entitled to pretend like you're one as well." He almost looked apologetic as he said his next words, though his effect didn't weaken. "Like I've said, I'm good at my job, and because of that, it doesn't matter whether or not I like you. I will charge you with hampering an investigation if you continue. You need to back off and leave this to the police."

"Were you even aware that Sid started the edible business? He was getting his marijuana from the Green Munchies in Lyons, and that Opal was the one who talked him out of it. Did you know it was Opal who decided they could make a lot more if they began growing their own product?" Whether it was due to my temper or needing to feel justified, the words fell from my lips before I could bring them back. I'd promised myself I wouldn't bring up that detail to anyone unless I had good reason to believe it could clear Barry's name. I didn't exactly know what the consequences would be, but I didn't want to be responsible for getting Eddie and his business in trouble, not with as kind as he was to Barry and myself. Not unless I had to.

Fury crossed Branson's face, and he gripped the soupspoon so tightly it trembled and clinked against the bowl. "What?"

"You heard me." I wasn't going to repeat it. I wasn't.

His nostrils flared as he spoke. "That little weasel was the one filtering drugs into *my* town?"

I wasn't completely sure why I felt protective of Eddie, but I did. "You're missing the point. Sid was the one who set up the operation, and then Opal took charge. Who knows what else she was doing, or how many enemies she made. The least of whom is Barry. And my point remains, I'm clearly discovering things the police department has no idea about, just by talking to people over a matter of days. So don't tell me to back off when I'm doing a better job of it than you are."

Branson had appeared muscular and strong in a model, man-in-uniform way before. But as he trembled with rage, that illusion faded. Combined with his anger, physical power seemed to radiate off him. And while I didn't feel necessarily unsafe with him; I wasn't entirely certain he was as predictable as I'd assumed.

After several tense moments, still trembling, Branson stood with clenched fists. "Thank you for dinner. And regardless of what you think about me, my abilities, or the Estes Park Police in general, you will leave this well enough alone. I will not hesitate to formally charge you, Fred. The best thing you can do to help your stepfather is to let us handle it. You will only get in the way."

I started to argue, but he was already storming toward the front door. Just as he touched the handle, he glanced back. Though unsuccessful, it seemed he was attempting to infuse some kindness into his tone. "The other reason I came was to tell you that we're done at Heads and Tails. Maybe it seems as if we've been sitting on our thumbs, but we've had a murder scene to deal with, as well as a grow house. We've been focusing our attention there. I knew it was important to you to get your business going." The accusation in his eyes was obvious. "So it's done. You can take possession of it again tomorrow." And with that, he was gone.

I sat there, stunned, too many emotions,

thoughts, and possibilities tumbling around in my mind and gut. After a while, I tossed what little remained of Branson's sandwich to Watson and took a bite of my own. Whatever he said, if he thought I was going to sit back and let the cards fall where they may regarding my family, he was sorely mistaken.

When I got up in the middle of the night to take Watson outside, this time on a leash, I was still so angry I promised myself I'd march right back downtown, barge into every single store, and become even more direct with my questioning. *Nobody* told me what to do. Not even a police officer.

By the time dawn crept through the windows, however, my temper had abated somewhat. I didn't have any follow-up questions to what little I'd discovered the day before, so it made more sense to wait. Selfishly, I wanted to get into my shop. To really spend some time there and begin to plan its future. The benefit was that I'd found I often thought more clearly when I was distracted with other work. Maybe in mapping out the layout of the Cozy Corgi, something in the back of my mind would click.

Packing a lunch of tomato soup and a freshly

made grilled cheese for myself and a baked chicken breast for Watson, we headed downtown again. By lunch, the soup and grilled cheese would be cold, but I thought I could manage. If I couldn't, there was a fully functioning kitchen upstairs. Just because a woman had been killed there didn't mean the stove couldn't heat up soup and grilled cheese.

I didn't bother with the leash in the short distance between my car and the shop, and no sooner had I opened the door than Watson took off like a bolt. Not a big deal; if he wanted to explore, he could. I flipped on the light downstairs and suddenly realized I could hear the pitter patter of his little feet above my head.

Of course he would go to the floor where we'd found a dead body.

I'd planned on working myself up to checking out the second floor again. But no time like the present. I supposed it didn't matter if Watson was up there or not. It wasn't like it was disrespectful, but it still didn't sit right. I marched up the steps and flicked on the light, illuminating the second story. He was nowhere to be seen.

"Watson?"

There was a snuffling, and he popped his head out the doorway of the kitchen.

Where else would he be? "Come here."

He let out a little whine, took a tentative step in my direction, then scampered around and disappeared once more.

"Good Lord, you are such a little brat." Might as well get it over with. I walked toward him, took a deep breath, chastised myself for being ridiculous, and stepped into the kitchen. "What are you doing in here? Looking for clues?"

Watson ignored me, scurrying here and there, his nose shoved to the floor. He hurried to the door, sniffed around it, both in the kitchen and outside in the main room, and then darted back into the kitchen once more.

Then it hit me. "You're looking for candy, aren't you? More of that licorice stuff you had last time." So much for clues. Well, I was already there, might as well look around. There was nothing to find. No chalk outline, no stain of blood, no rolling pin—not that I'd expected there to be. It also didn't look like the aftermath left from an inspection. The place was spotless. Even the appliances looked like they'd gotten wiped down, not even a trace from where they'd surely dusted for fingerprints. Now that I thought about it, I realized the same had been true for downstairs. The place was remarkably cleaner than the first time I'd seen it.

My irritation at Branson lessened further. I had no doubt it was thanks to him.

The kitchen wasn't anything special. Though more updated than the one at my house, it lacked any amount of charm. And despite Opal creating her edibles here, none of the equipment was high quality. I looked down at the floor where I'd found Opal's body. I could still see her lying there.

"I'm going to figure out who killed you, Opal. Although, let's be honest, I'm doing it for Barry more than I am for you." That was an understatement. "I am sorry for your loss. But just so we're clear, I'm using the kitchen to warm up my lunch later on. If you have a problem with it, you better start haunting me now."

Sorry for your loss? Is that what you should say to someone who'd been murdered?

And if that thought wasn't enough to let me know I needed to be elsewhere, I didn't know what was. I realized I still had my bag in my hand, so I went over to the refrigerator and put in my soup, the sandwich, and Watson's chicken.

I gave Watson the cold shoulder as I walked out of the kitchen, not that he minded. "I'm going to eat your lunch, by the way. Good luck finding candy." I wouldn't do it of course, but it would serve him right.

After returning downstairs, I decided to get all the unpleasant tasks over with, so I looked in the storeroom. I was certain the deep freezer would be empty. To my surprise, the freezer was gone. That seemed a little presumptuous. Maybe they'd seized it for evidence, and I'd get it back once they were done? After another moment of consideration, I decided to tell Branson to dispose of the thing, if possible, the next time I saw him. It wasn't like I'd keep food or anything in it. I'd never be able to open the lid and not see a dead owl staring up at me.

I wandered from tiny room to tiny room that surrounded the large open space in the center. Once again my excitement built as I pictured how charming the place was going to be. Even if it was dreary and rather depressing at the moment.

But I could fix that part easily enough.

As I walked to the windows, I considered. Everyone would be staring in, trying to catch a glimpse of the place Opal Garble was murdered, or to get a look at the woman who found her. Well, whatever. Just like with the kitchen, might as well get it over with. In less than five minutes, I'd ripped down all the paper covering the windows, and the morning sunlight filtered in, brightening up the place.

If I hadn't been excited before, I was then. The shop almost glowed in all its wooden wonder. There was some damage from where taxidermy had been hung and age spots here and there, but nothing that endless bookcases wouldn't fix.

Whatever irritation I still held against Branson faded away with him giving me the gift of getting in here quickly. I truly was ready to begin my new life. So ready, I had a moment's thankfulness to Charlotte for stabbing me in the back. I shook the thought off quickly. I most definitely didn't owe her any gratefulness. But the end result was enough money I could live on, if I was frugal, for the rest of my life. And Lord knew, there was no other way a person should open a physical book-shop in this day and age. Still, she'd stolen my career, and even though the settlement was substantial, it was nothing compared to what the publishing house would make by the time we hit retirement.

A friendly round face smiled at me from the window, startling me and ushering me back to the present. I'd been so caught in the past, it took me a moment to recognize who was waving at me. When I did, I hurried to the front door and let her in. "Katie!

What are you doing here?" Dumb question. "Taking a break from the shop?"

Katie stepped inside. Before I could shut the door, Watson let out a torrent of barks from upstairs and then barreled down the steps, probably preparing for an intruder. He barked a couple more times, then pulled to a stop when Katie knelt and held out the back of her hand. With a sniff, he inspected, nudged her fingers with his nose in way of approval, and padded off once more. She smiled at me as she stood. "He's not the most affectionate of little guys, is he?"

"Not hardly. Although he is with some people." I rolled my eyes as I noticed him disappear back up the steps. He was determined, I'd give him that, at least where food was concerned. "He's even affectionate with me at times. Typically when I have food. But he's captured my heart, the little monster. He thinks I'm here to serve him. Which, at times, I think is right."

"Well, he's cute, that's for sure." She glanced around, scrutinizing, then returned to me. "No, the shops aren't open yet. Everything's up in the air." She sighed. "It's part of why I came downtown. I had to get out of the house. Then I saw the paper was down from the windows. I thought I'd say hi, see how you're doing."

For a heartbeat, I wondered if Katie was doing some of her own investigation, then realized I was being paranoid. "That's sweet of you. I'm doing fine. Glad to be able to get back in here. It's going to take a while to get everything set up, but I think it will end up being beautiful. A cozy little bookshop."

"It's a great place. And it'll be a lot better now that it's not filled with taxidermy."

I shuddered. "At least the bar is set low."

Katie fidgeted, nervous. She licked her lips before speaking again. "You redheads are able to wear the most god-awful colors and look wonderful. I simply don't understand it."

I wasn't sure what I'd been expecting, but most definitely not that. "Excuse me?"

She made a waving motion over my body. "You've got on a mustard-colored sweater over a pea-green and drab-brown speckled skirt. All of which are colors of baby vomit. And yet somehow, it makes your skin glow and your hair practically shine."

She was right. Earth tones were most definitely my color, but still. "Uhm, thank you. I think."

"Take me, for instance. If I put on any one of those colors, I'd instantly look sick, like I was dying. I have to stick to blues and greens and other jewel tones. Luckily, they're my favorite anyway, so it doesn't matter."

What in the world was happening? "Well, your skin is already tanned and glowing the way it is, so I suppose that makes sense."

She nodded. "I'm of Sicilian heritage." Her gaze flicked around the shop. "We have good skin."

"Katie." I opted for bluntness. "What's going on? It's nice of you to come by and say hi, but we've entered this weird conversation of colors and fashion which I'm not really sure what to do with."

She practically sighed in relief. "Ah, you're right. I'm so sorry. I've just been starved for adult conversation. Anything. Even if it's only about your horrible choice in colors." She waved over my body again. "Not that you don't look absolutely wonderful in them. But I needed to talk to someone who could offer some sort of mental stimulation greater than a five-year-old. I've been staying with Lois since Opal's death, and I'm afraid I'm just a little... desperate."

"It's nice of you to stay with Lois during this hard time." Katie had spoken so fast I had to replay some of the finer points before I could take in their meaning. "If I'm not mistaken, I was placing Lois to be quite a bit older than a five-year-old."

Katie rolled her eyes. "I would've thought so too. I've worked around her for two years, and I had no idea she was like she is." She bugged her eyes. "I have a whole new respect for Opal, and that's saying something. If I'd been Opal, it probably would have been Lois you found dead up there."

What a strange thing to say. Lois... and what a thought. An interesting one. "Well, you've got me now. Want to have a seat and tell me about it?" I motioned toward the folding chairs Branson and I had sat on just a few days ago.

"Oh, no, I couldn't dream of it. I know you've got a billion things to do." Even as she spoke she headed toward the chairs and plopped down. "But if you have a second, I won't turn it down. I'm sure it's horrible to make a joke like this, but you might just be saving me from murder."

I sat in the other chair across from her. I desperately wanted to hear what Katie had to say. As scattered as she was, it felt important, but the way we were seemed a little awkward. Like a police investigation or something. "We can go up to the kitchen. There might be tea or something to eat up there. If nothing else, I have some tomato soup we could share. If that docsn't make you too nervous."

Katie looked at me puzzled. "Why would that make me nervous?"

"Well... the kitchen is where I found Opal."

Her eyes brightened. "Oh! Right! That's where Opal was making all her edible pastries and things. Maybe there's still some supplies up there." She was beginning to sound like I'd just given her a Christmas present. "Do you mind if I bake something while we chat? I'll do something easy and quick. While living with Lois, I've not been allowed to make anything outside of vegan recipes that don't allow any sugar." She shook her head. "No sugar!"

Some of the affection I felt for her before returned. She was a strange woman, but I liked her immensely. "Absolutely. I love that you're not timid about being in the same room where a woman died, and I suppose you're offering to share whatever you make?"

"Of course!" With that, Katie practically launched from her chair, and though unintentional, did a nearly spot-on impression of Watson as she bounded up the stairs.

As I suspected, all ingredients had been stripped bare. Katie said the same was true for Opal's shop.

Proving just how desperate she was, Katie made a run to the grocery store and was elbow deep in flour and powdered sugar as she made the crust for lemon bars.

I liked Katie already, but I was fairly certain that by the end of the baking process, I would practically be in love with the woman. I gave her a chance to lose herself in the process before I began questioning. "So tell me, what's so horrible about living with Lois? She seems like such a sweet old lady."

"She is! She's a darling little lamb." Katie spoke freely as she measured, then poured powdered sugar into the mixer. "But that said, she is one intense little lamb."

Funny, Katie was the second person to compare Lois to a lamb.

She motioned down to Watson, who hadn't left her side since she started baking. "She's quite literally been so under my feet that I practically keep tripping over her. She's always been nice to me, but it's like we're suddenly best friends or sisters." She angled a telltale glance my way. "*Conjoined* sisters more like."

Katie chuckled at her own joke, and I chimed in. Lois definitely sounded more intense than I would've expected, but she'd been fairly shattered when she'd come into Victorian Antlers two days before, so maybe it was to be expected. "She does seem rather fragile. Don't you imagine she's just afraid to be alone?"

"I'm sure that's it, of course it is. And I feel horrible being critical. But I haven't had a moment to myself. Thank the Lord she had a hair appointment, and those always take her hours."

I started to nod, then hesitated. "Her hair appointments take hours? I could see that for Opal, not for Lois. Her hair looks natural."

Katie rolled her eyes. "It is. But it's still a process. Believe me, I've heard about it in detail. She goes to this homeopathic hairdresser. First there's an oatmeal bath, next they do something with mayonnaise, but it's the homemade, egg-free kind, of course. After that—"

"Okay, I got it. That makes sense. Sort of." I winked at her. "If you're really conjoined twins all of the sudden, I'm surprised you're not getting an oatmeal treatment for yourself."

She shivered. "Oh, she tried. Even broke down and cried a little bit. But I had to put my foot down at something." Katie fingered her spiral locks, leaving a trace of flour behind. "My hair was that something. But you would've thought I was killing her. I'm telling you, Fred. I take back every bad thought and word I've ever had about Opal. No wonder she was angry all the time. Lois is sweet, but the woman is possessive! I dated a guy like that once, for about two weeks. Worst two weeks of my life. It's like she owns me."

I couldn't even fathom it, but a horrible thought entered my head. "Did you know Opal and Sid were dating?"

Katie smacked both her dirty hands down on the counter and gaped at me. "You're kidding? Opal hated him." She glanced around the kitchen. "Although, I didn't know she was making edibles either, and if she was doing it in Sid's kitchen... who knows? Opal acted like she hated everyone except for Lois. And I've heard she'd been married several times, so maybe it was just her idea of romance."

Katie popped a small glass pan into the oven and returned to the mixer and began beating some eggs, before looking up at me suddenly. "Where did you hear about Opal and Sid? I never would've suspected."

"From the guy who owns the Green Munchies in Lyons. I drove down to talk to him the day before yesterday." I wasn't sure if it was residual from my conversation with Branson the night before or not, but as I made my admission to Katie, I was surprised to find myself a little embarrassed. "I've been asking around. I thought maybe I could find something that would help clear Barry's name."

To my surprise, Katie cocked her jaw and grinned. "Doesn't surprise me at all. No wonder I like you." She let out a girlish laugh, one that didn't quite fit her. "I actually went and saw Eddie myself yesterday."

"You did?"

She nodded. "Yes. I snuck out of the house for a couple of hours. Came back to Lois being a complete sobbing mess. I can't even say why I went there, but I just felt so stupid, all this coming to light and it's been right under my nose. I know people think that I knew about it, about Opal making edibles. But I swear I didn't. Lois didn't either. She's completely devastated. I just needed to know how big a fool I'd been to not notice. Eddie was sweet. Assured me the way things had been set up, there would've been no way I could've known. And he didn't have one good thing to say about Opal."

"Tell me about it." Guilt bit at me at the thought of Eddie. I had no doubt that I'd caused him some sort of trouble with what I'd told Branson. Maybe I'd drive down later in the afternoon and apologize. Or give him warning.

"Did you know a few years ago, in North

Carolina, a bunch of newborns were testing positive for being addicted to marijuana?"

Katie's question was so out of the blue it drove Eddie out of my thoughts. It was almost as though she was trying to distract me. "You know, I can't say I did know that."

Katie nodded sagely as she zested a lemon. "It's true. And then the nurses would have to call social services, of course, because the newborns had to have become addicted to marijuana from someone, and it had to be their mothers, obviously." She looked at me expectantly.

"Obviously." If she was playing me, her acting skills were stellar, and I couldn't shake my innate sense of fondness for the woman.

"Well—" Katie dipped a finger in the bright yellow mixture, stuck it into her mouth, and gave a pleased smile. "—it turns out, that none of those baby mamas were using drugs of any kind. After an investigation, they discovered certain brands of baby soaps and shampoos, while not actually getting the babies high at all or even containing THC, were causing the babies to give false positive on drugs tests."

I waited for the story to continue. It didn't. "Oh, that's... something."

Katie nodded again. "I know, right."

Again I hesitated, but no further explanation was offered. "Katie, does that have something to do with Opal?"

"I don't think so." She seemed to consider as she removed the crust from the oven, then peered over at me expectantly. "Do you?"

I shook my head, trying not to laugh. "I doubt it, but I thought maybe you did since you brought it up."

"No, that was just a little tidbit about marijuana for you." She shrugged. "Sometimes, when I get a topic on my mind, I do a lot of research. Granted, with Lois over my shoulder, I've not been able to do as much as I normally would, but I managed a little. It was just one of the interesting stories I found out."

"Well, okay then. You never know when you might need a random fact. They might make all the difference." The lady was a hoot.

Katie poured the lemon mixture over the baked crust, and shoved it into the oven with a contented sigh. "I can't thank you enough, Fred. I almost feel like myself again."

"I'm the one who should be thanking you. I get fresh-baked goodness, have a pleasant memory in this kitchen, and someone to bounce ideas off of." It would be silly to say out loud, but I truly did feel like

I'd made my first friend in town. "And maybe this sounds horrible, but as nice as it is to do what you're doing for Lois, surely you can't take it all upon yourself to stay with her. That's too much for any person. Even if it was a role Opal filled for her."

Instant guilt cut across Katie's features, and embarrassment weighted down her tone. "I have a confession." I lifted my eyebrows, and she continued. "Commercial rental property isn't easy to come by in Estes. Especially the kind I need, since I'm a baker. Opal and Lois are listed jointly on both shops' leases, Sinful Bites and Healthy Delights. I'm hoping Lois will let me take over Opal's side of the lease. I can finally open my own bakery like I've dreamed." She grimaced. "I truly did like Lois, and I'm sure I will again when I don't want to strangle her, but the lease is one of the main reasons I'm still staying with Lois. That makes me horrible, doesn't it?"

I laughed. "For some reason, Katie dear, it makes me like you even more." It was true. But, it also could be a reason for Katie to want Opal out of the way. Though I simply couldn't see Katie doing such a thing.

She beamed in relief, but her eyes widened, and she turned and set the timer above the oven. "Barely remembered." She moved to the sink and began to wash up as she continued to speak. "Any other fun factoid you'd like to know about marijuana? I discovered a ton. I can even tell you what wattage of lights is best for optimal growth."

I sat up straighter, Katie's words triggering something. "I forgot, I haven't checked out the basement, where Opal and Sid were growing all their product. Barry said it was nothing more than a crawl space." I motioned to the door. "Want to check it out with me?"

"You know I do!" She gave little more than a cursory wipe of her hands with the dishtowel, and we hurried down to the main floor.

Near the back, in a hallway close to the storage room, another door led down to a long flight of steps. I flicked the light switch by the doorframe, and we wandered down. I gaped as we arrived into a huge room, nearly half the floor space of the level above, with the ceiling two inches above my head. I lifted my hand, touching the underside of the floorboards of the main level. "They've put some work into this place. Maybe Barry didn't remember, but a crawl-space definitely doesn't have six-foot ceilings." The room was empty, nothing but the lights overhead, no trace of plants, pot or otherwise. A tingle of excitement went through me, and I looked over at Katie.

"You want to hear what makes *me* a horrible person?"

A smile spread across her face, and she nodded.

"I love that whatever Opal and Sid did, they did all the backbreaking work, and I now have an actual storage room."

THIRTEEN

Katie cut the cooled lemon bars and sprinkled powdered sugar over the top before choosing four of them to bring over.

"It's a good thing I'm not a salad kind of girl. There's gotta be two days' worth of calories in this thing." I picked up one of the lemon bars, sniffed it, and managed to offer up a cloud of powdered sugar which combined with the snow lightly falling outside the window and made a perfect holiday moment, despite all of the turmoil.

Katie chuckled. "Nah. I almost made my ginger-bread recipe, which I serve with ice cream. Lemon bars almost count as dessert."

I started to laugh, but the sound turned into an awkward orgasmic groan as I took a bite. Bright, tart, and sweet, and even better than it smelled. "Oh my God. I think I'm in love with you."

"Just wait until you try more of my savory dishes.

They're my specialty." She giggled. "You'll be asking me to marry you."

"I'm close to that already." I took another bite; it was just as good as the first.

Watson had already devoured his chicken, and was staring up at us expectantly. I pretended not to notice.

"Do you think it says horrible things about us, when we're able to enjoy eating in here where Opal passed?"

Katie shrugged. "Not at all. The kitchen is for cooking and eating. Not for killing someone. Or for dying, for that matter. It's the killer and Opal who made the faux pas, not us." She took another huge bite as if to prove her point.

"All right, seriously now, where have you been my entire life?"

"If I told you, I'd have to kill you." She started to giggle and then cut herself off. "Okay, even I have to admit that's a little too far."

Our gazes met over our perfect desserts, and we both burst out laughing. God, it felt good to laugh. Felt good to be normal and happy. A wave of affection washed over me, and I reached out to squeeze Katie's forearm. "Thank you for this. I can't tell you how much I needed it. It feels like I haven't laughed in ages."

"You've been under a lot of stress since the moment you moved into town. I'd say that's understandable."

"It's been a lot longer than that." A hint of shadow filtered back into my mind. "Part of why I came here to begin with. So thank you."

A pleased blush rose to Katie's cheeks, and she smiled. "I'm thankful too. Trust me, there weren't any moments like this with Opal. Whatever brought you to town, I'm glad you're here." She started to take another bite, then paused. "Still... I must admit, I'm curious why you chose Estes Park. I know your mom is here, but we don't get many single women in the prime of their lives moving to Estes."

"You're here, aren't you?"

Her kind eyes flashed panic, and for the first time, her smile seemed forced. She shook her head, curls bobbing. Despite what I noticed, when she spoke, Katie was back to her normal, cheerful self. "Oh no you don't. This is about you, and I asked first." Her brown eyes sparkled. "And I told you when I'm curious about things, I like to find out stuff. So far, I've discovered you founded your own publishing company. Is your bookstore an offshoot of that or something?"

For a moment I was thrown off at the thought of Katie researching me on the internet. Then I remembered her odd factoids about marijuana. Maybe this was just part of Katie.

She backpedaled quickly. "Not that you have to tell me, of course. I'm sure it's none of my business."

It wasn't any of her business, but suddenly, I needed it to be. Or at least needed to share with someone who wasn't obligated to take my side through the bonds of family. There was something off about Katie, or something she was hiding. Maybe it made me as big a fool as Barry with Gerald, but I couldn't shake the feeling that I could trust her. "No, it's okay. I can talk about it. And no, the bookshop is not an offshoot of the publishing house. My partner and I had a falling out. I'm no longer a part of the company."

Katie hesitated like she was judging if she should ask the next question or not, but I already knew her well enough to know that she would ask whatever it was. Sure enough, she proved me right. "I have to say, I'm surprised. Honestly, my guess was that you'd gone through a divorce. Felt the need to have a life switch or something."

"You're closer than you know." Goodness, was I that much of a stereotype? Single woman moving across the country to start her life anew. "The divorce was six years ago. It's the other version of the tale as old as time. Husband replaces his wife for a younger model, complete with *enhanced* features."

Katie chuckled, but more in commiseration than humor. "I can just imagine."

"I did a life change then too." Yes, it seemed I truly was a stereotype, in duplicate. Might as well own it. "I was a college professor, specializing in American and British literature. After the affair, I left teaching. My childhood best friend, Charlotte, and I joined together and opened a publishing house. To both our surprises, within a year, it was a smashing success. To this day, I can't tell you why, when so many other small publishing houses are closing. Maybe just dumb luck. Whatever it was, those six years working with Charlotte were the best of my life. I was honestly grateful Garrett had the affair and wanted a divorce. It made my life so much better." A sense of loss cut through me. I really had built such a beautiful life. I hadn't wanted anything more.

"I'm sorry, Fred." This time Katie reached across with the companionable squeeze. She let a few moments pass before asking more questions. "You said you and Charlotte had a falling out?"

I couldn't hold back a bitter laugh. "That was a polite way for me to put it. It turned out, I was a fool, and Charlotte found fortune much more enticing than friendship."

"No!" Katie's tone grew defensive. "Don't refer to yourself like that. Just because someone is a horrible person, doesn't make you a fool."

"In this case, it does. Long story short, Charlotte was better with the numbers. I was better with the creatives. It was part of what made us such a great team. She handled contracts and finances. I handled going over submissions and choosing the writers and books I thought had the best chance of being successful. We were both extremely good at what we did. She'd formatted our business agreements in such a way, from the very beginning, that when the time came, it was easy to push me to the side. I should've had a separate lawyer look over our contracts when we founded the company. But she was my best friend. It never entered my mind she only had her own interest at heart. A much larger publishing house came along and wanted to incorporate us into their business. I resisted, not realizing I didn't have much of a say. Now Charlotte and our company are part of the big five, and I'm here, opening a bookshop."

Katie looked furious. "You should sue!"

I laughed again, once more there was no humor. "The past nine months have been nothing more than litigation. But that's part of why I showed up so much sooner than expected. All of the sudden, I was just done. I could see the lawsuit spreading out for the next years of my life. It's no way to live. So I settled. For a very good chunk of money, to be sure, but nothing compared to what should have been." I motioned around the kitchen. "I can't say I'm glad it happened, but I *am* glad I'm here. And I'm excited about what the Cozy Corgi will become. I'm ready for a simple, beautiful, easy life. Just Watson and me, my family, my bookstore, a beautiful mountain town —" I gave Katie a heartfelt smile. "—new friends. The perfect life. True, a different version than what I had envisioned. But who knows, maybe it will be a better one."

"I hope so." Katie returned my smile, but then hers became teasing. "Not to be a naysayer, but I'm not sure what it says when your new adventure begins with a murder. I'm impressed you're still here. I think I would've tossed my little bundle of fur in the back seat and got myself right back down the mountain."

This time, my tone was genuine once more. "Like I said. It seems I like to play the part of a fool. And even though there are no books yet, I'm going to fight for this little place. Whatever it takes, I'm going to make it work. You wait and see. The Cozy Corgi is going to be the best little bookshop you've ever seen in your life."

"You know, Fred, I don't doubt you in the least." She eyed my empty plate. I didn't even remember finishing it. "Want another piece?"

"Are you kidding? The first two were the size of small icebergs."

"Well, I want a third." She narrowed her eyes. "I think you should have another, just to make sure that ex-husband and ex-best friend of yours know you're going to enjoy every second of your new life."

Who could argue with that? I slid the plate forward. "Fill me up, my friend. This new life doesn't come with the calorie counter!"

I enjoyed my time with Katie so much I nearly suggested she stay as I continued making plans for the layout of the shop. I didn't. Not because I didn't trust or like Katie, but I needed this store to be my own. For better or worse, I wanted every decision to be mine. No more business partner. This shop would be entirely Winifred Wendy Page, and no one else. Well, no one else besides Watson in any case.

Between the early hour of sunset, thanks to winter, and me losing track of time, it was dark by the time Watson and I left the Cozy Corgi.

After my time with Katie, Eddie continued to be on my mind. I didn't count him a friend, definitely not in the same way I did Katie, but I truly did feel guilty about selling him out to Branson so quickly. Or maybe the emotion had very little to do with Katie and revolved more around Charlotte. Not the same thing by any means, but it was most definitely not the type of person I wanted to be.

Though the early evening was dark, it had quit snowing, and the roads were clear. I was halfway to Lyons when I realized I should've at least called. I had noticed Green Munchies stayed open until ten every evening, but it didn't mean Eddie would be there. As there was no cell reception between Estes Park and Lyons, Watson and I just kept going.

We arrived a little past six thirty. Once again, I didn't bother with a leash, so Watson followed me up the sidewalk and into the front door. Like before, the place was sleek and clean, the massive plastic ovals casting a soft glow through the place. Eddie was nowhere to be seen. No one was anywhere to be seen. Other than soft music, the place was silent.

I nearly called out, but didn't want to be rude, so I decided to wait. Instead of going to the edibles like we had before, I wandered around the other section of the shop, checking out the various paraphernalia, most of which I was clueless to what they were.

The assortment of pipes was rather fascinating, ranging from simple clear glass to intricate ones shaped like dragons and fairies. My favorite was a combination of glass and metal, complete with wheels and dials, designed in a steampunk style. It looked more like a piece of art than a pipe. I'd have to ask Eddie to show me if the wheels and gadgets actually did anything or if they were just for show.

As I perused the store, a tingle of anxiety began to gnaw at me. Something was off. "Eddie?"

Watson flinched at the sudden sound of my voice. Strangely, it was even startling to me. Things were too quiet.

Not pausing to consider, I stepped behind the counter and headed toward the door that to led into the back. "Eddie?"

The lights were on but dim, revealing a small

stockroom with a warehouse feel. Like the front of the shop, it was clean, modern, and organized. Still no movement or sound.

"Eddie?"

Watson whimpered and lowered his head. With a whine, he glanced up at me, then returned his attention to the ground. He headed off in the direction I'd just noticed. A door in the back wall. Watson reached it a few paces before me, paused with his nose pressed to the crack of the door, and let out a low growl.

I reached for the door handle and hesitated. What was I doing? Playing the part of a fool, to be sure. There'd already been one murder in a dispensary; now here I was, in another one, alone.

For some reason, whether it be stupidity or stubbornness, the idea of rushing back to the car and calling the police seemed weak. I gripped the door handle, turned it, and gave a push.

The room was dark but a newly familiar odor hung in the air.

The volume of Watson's growl increased.

Hand trembling, I felt beside the doorframe, found the light switch, and flicked it on.

This time when I found a dead body, I didn't gasp. Somehow, I'd expected it.

Eddie lay facedown on the office floor. His feet were nearest me, and I couldn't see his face, but I knew it was Eddie, even without confirming his handlebar mustache. Although different, his clothes nearly matched what he'd worn before. If not on the floor, his tall, lean frame could almost have passed for being asleep, his arms and legs straight and relaxed. Blood matted the back of his head, and a large pool had grown around him. Some insane part of me demanded that I go to him and check to make sure he was dead.

Maybe I didn't gasp, but I couldn't bring myself to touch him either. There was nothing to check. I'd never seen a gunshot wound, but I was certain that was what I was looking at, and something about the blood made me feel like he'd been dead for a little while at least.

Still growling, Watson slinked toward him, sniffing at the soles of Eddie's shoes.

I smacked my thigh. "No! Stay back, boy." Once again, the volume of my words startled both of us, and I froze. Here I was being loud with a dead body at my feet. What if the killer was still around?

No sooner had the thought flitted through my mind than I tossed it away. If there was anyone else here, I would've heard them while I was in the front room.

Not taking the chance that Watson was going to get into one of his stubborn streaks, I scooped him into my arms, carried him to the car, and got inside. I dialed 911 and told them I would wait for them outside the shop.

Poor Eddie. Poor, poor Eddie. The only person who seemed to be grieving about Opal was Lois. Somehow, I knew that wouldn't be true for Eddie.

In a crazy thought, a part of me was relieved he wouldn't be getting into trouble from Branson. He wouldn't know that I'd so easily thrown him under the bus. I shook my head at the thought. What a horrible notion.

One thing was for sure, though. With Eddie's death, it most definitely narrowed the motive. This didn't have anything to do with dead husbands or owl feathers. I supposed it might still be connected to blackmail, but I couldn't see Eddie being involved in that.

Part of me wished Barry hadn't been released on bail after all. Then, at least it would've been simple to prove he hadn't committed this murder either.

FOURTEEN

"I'm telling you, Sergeant Wexler couldn't have been nicer." Barry paused from where he was scrubbing the wall. He kept forgetting to wring out his sponge after dipping it into the sudsy water, and as a result, his pink-and-blue tie-dye shirt was nearly soaked from the mess running down his arm. "When he came by the house this morning, it was like he'd never truly thought I'd done it at all."

I didn't really believe Branson had thought Barry killed Opal. Which was part of my frustration with him. He hadn't come to the Green Munchies the night before, so I hadn't been able to get a feel from him on what he was going to do about Barry.

Mom looked over from where she was sponging the opposite wall, without halfway drowning herself. "Well, of course not. No one in their right mind would think you could hurt anyone. And he *should* be nice. All the trouble he put us through. I'm just glad we had an alibi for that drug dealer's death in Lyons."

"His name was Eddie, Mom. He was a nice guy." I still felt a twinge of guilt at the thought of Eddie. Though the notion made no sense. There was nothing I could've done. But still, while Katie and I had been gossiping over freshly baked lemon bars, Eddie was being shot.

"Yes, he was." Barry cocked an eyebrow my direction. "You thought so too, Fred?" At his feet, Watson pranced through a puddle of water, leaving footprints trailing behind him.

"Watson!" Percival's cry was a little shrill. "I just finished mopping."

"I told you to save mopping till last." Gary shook a putty knife in Percival's direction, then transferred the piece of candy he was sucking to the other cheek before speaking again. "I'm going to leave a mess behind after I scrape the putty off these patches when they're dry. And I don't want to hear a word about it."

"Fred said she didn't care about the holes. They're going to be covered by bookcases anyway." Percival and Gary had been bickering since they arrived with my parents to the Cozy Corgi over an hour before.

"Okay, you two. I don't want to be responsible for the bookstore causing quarrels." I refocused on Barry, more to avoid further sniping than any desire to continue to talk about Eddie. "Granted, I only met him that once, but Eddie seemed very sweet. And he absolutely loved you."

Mom let out a long-suffering sigh. "Well, he should. Barry informed me just how frequent his trips to Lyons were and how extremely unfrugal they could be."

Barry muttered something under his breath.

The four of them had insisted on doing a deep clean now we had the store back. The process made much easier by Branson and the police department. Before Mom could retort, I switched the conversation again. "So you feel like Branson—Sergeant Wexler truly believed your alibi?"

Mom answered for them. "The four of us were having our monthly spades tournament yesterday. We were all together. So Barry has three alibis."

"I'm surprised he didn't find that a little too convenient." Was that irritation I was feeling? I thought so, but the term didn't feel quite right.

Percival grinned at me from where he followed Watson around with the mop. It seemed Watson was enjoying the game. "You can quit calling him

Sergeant Wexler, darling. We all know the two of you are on a first-name basis. And now he's not threatening to lock up your stepfather forever, I'm certain you have the entire family's blessing to take that hot man on a date!"

Before I could protest, Barry joined in. "I think you should. He obviously likes you. He even asked about you this morning. Wanted to know if you were okay after discovering Eddie's body."

"He did?"

Barry nodded.

And with that, I realized *irritation* hadn't been the right word for what I was feeling. I was hurt. Branson knew I discovered Eddie's body, he had to be aware I'd be worried about the police trying to pin a second murder on my stepfather, and he hadn't so much as called.

The realization made me want to hurry over and pick up Barry's bucket of dirty water and dump it over my head. I had no business feeling hurt, or any other sentiment, for Branson Wexler. "Well, I'll believe it when I see it. It wouldn't surprise me at all if he swings by here any minute to take you in for further questioning."

"He won't. He was very clear that as far as he was concerned, the case against Barry was closed."

Mom dropped the sponge into her bucket, wiped her hands on her jeans, and crossed the room to pat my cheek. "It's over, sweetie. And I can't thank you enough for all you tried to do for Barry. You are most definitely your father's daughter. But you can relax now. It really is done. Sergeant Wexler said he couldn't give us details of course, but that Eddie's murder had to be linked to Opal's. They were both involved in some shady business and must've made a common enemy." She dropped her hand and offered a sweet smile. "Percival is right. Branson is a very handsome man and obviously a very good cop, just like your father was. I think he would suit you."

I knew Mom was desperate for me to have another relationship. See me as happy as Barry's daughters were with their husbands and children. As much as she was thrilled I was in Estes taking over my grandparents' old cabin and opening the book-shop, I knew she didn't believe I was really fine on my own. And as far as the case being closed....

"I was thinking that way, too, last night. About Opal's murder and Eddie's being connected... not about Branson." I cast a warning glance at Percival, who had lifted a finger toward me and looked on the verge of a sermon. "But the more I think about it, the less it makes sense. None of you saw the bodies.

They were different, completely. Eddie was shot in the back of the head. His body was lying there like he was asleep. Opal was beaten with a rolling pin, for crying out loud. She was sprawled on the floor. If it was really drug-related, and if the same person killed her, why in the world would they use a rolling pin if they had a gun handy?"

Four pairs of blank eyes stared back at me. Clearly the thought hadn't occurred to any of them.

Gary pulled a piece of candy out of his pocket, causing Watson to hurry over at the sound of unwrapping cellophane, and he popped it into his mouth before offering a comment. "That's a good point, Fred. But you accomplished what you set out to do. Barry is no longer under suspicion. The police can handle it from here." He smiled at me, his affection clear. "Your job now, is to turn this empty store into the most adorable and cozy of all bookshops the world has ever seen. That's it."

How wonderful that sounded. If only it were that simple. "I hardly think I accomplished anything with Barry. I never cleared his name. It was just happenstance."

"You discovered Eddie." Barry beamed at me. "That led to clearing me."

"That would've happened anyway. Someone

would've found him. It didn't have to be me." I wished it hadn't been. For whatever reason, after discovering Opal's body, I had to make a choice to recall the scene. With Eddie, the sight of his lifeless body kept flashing behind my eyes.

"Well, either way, it's over. And we're all safe and sound. I call that a success." Mom gestured up the steps. "I'm glad you decided to get a refinisher here to do the floors before you have the bookcases installed. I think you should do upstairs too, while you're at it, even though you're not sure you want to extend the bookstore up there. At least that way it's done, and you'll have more options."

It took some effort to focus on the bookshop. "You're probably right. Might as well do it all the first time, just in case."

"Good." Mom clapped her hands. "Well then, Percival, I think we're about done here after you get one more pass with the mop, if we can get Watson to sit still, that is. I say we all go home and have dinner. I have a huge pan of enchiladas in the fridge, just waiting to be popped in the oven."

"Oh sure, leave all the backbreaking work to the older brother. I see how it is." Percival winked at Mom. "But you've got Grandma's recipe for enchiladas, so you know I'll do about anything for those."

Gary fished another piece of candy out of his pocket, but it slipped through his fingers and bounced across the floor. Watson scrambled for it.

"Oh no you don't!" To both of our surprises, I made it there first and snatched it from between his teeth. I grinned at him in satisfaction. "You're going to have to up your game, little one." I started to hand the candy to Gary, then stared at it, something trying desperately to click in my mind.

"You okay, darling?" Gary pulled another from his pocket and held it out to me. "You can have a fresh one."

"No, thank you. It's just that...." And then it snapped. Licorice. I looked up at Gary. "Where did you get this?"

"We have about a billion of these back at Victoria Antlers." He rolled his eyes. "Lois keeps bringing us a new basket of candy every single day. We've thrown everything away so far, except for these. These little hard licorice balls are the one thing the dear woman ever made that are any good. Maybe the only thing in my life that doesn't have sugar which was worth eating."

I stared at the licorice. Lois....

I refocused on Gary and then cast my gaze

around at the rest of my family. "Did Opal make these too?"

It was Barry who answered. "No. She didn't make hard candy of any kind. Not even her edibles. It was one of my complaints about buying from her. You either had to consume them quickly or freeze them. Which is fine, but if you freeze things, then you have to plan ahead to defrost them. Things like these are much easier to just unwrap and pop in your mouth without"—his gaze darted guiltily to Mom— "people knowing."

My heart began drumming out a rocketing rhythm, and I held the candy like it was a piece of evidence in the courtroom. "This is what Watson was eating the morning I found Opal's body. The one he got was from outside the kitchen door, right upstairs. And then there were others inside the kitchen as well."

I'd expected gasps of awe and understanding, but again, those four pairs of eyes stared at me expectantly, without any spark of comprehension.

I shook the candy at them. "You said yourself Opal never made these. And Lois said that she had no idea Opal was making edibles or using this kitchen." Still no reaction other than staring. I shook the candy again. "If Lois is the only one who makes these, then what were they doing in the kitchen when Opal was murdered?"

Flames of understanding began to flicker, but just barely. Gary's low voice was only just audible as he considered his words. "Could be just like what happened here. Maybe Opal had some in her pocket like I did and spilled them."

The others nodded in agreement. And I had to admit, it made sense. But not quite. "I got the impression Opal didn't like Lois's baking." I was certain I wasn't making that up, but I wasn't sure if I'd actually heard someone say it or if it was just what little I'd seen of how Opal treated her sister.

"I doubt she did. There's not much to like. But maybe she liked these." Gary shrugged again. "Trust me, it helps to have something you genuinely like to be able to brag about when Lois is around."

Mom came up and slipped her arm into mine. "Let the police handle it, honey. I'm sure everything is fine. Let's wrap up here and go home to dinner."

FIFTEEN

Giving an excuse that I needed to stay and do a couple more things upstairs, which I didn't think anyone believed, I sent the family on their way with the promise that I would be at Mom's shortly.

I needed to think. Without other voices around.

Though I couldn't quite make sense of all the puzzle pieces, my gut told me I was right about Lois. I couldn't truly picture her doing it, but now that the thought had entered my mind, I couldn't quite *not* see her doing it either.

But what to do?

Watson followed me as I paced, and after a couple of circles around the shop, I realized we were leaving footprints in Percival's mop job. I took a second to feel guilty about that, then wondered why we'd bothered with mopping at all. I was going to have the floors refinished.

I shoved the thought away, not important and

obviously not the point, and continued pacing. My family was wrong. Even if I couldn't explain why. They just were. For whatever reason, it had been Lois. As soon as I saw that licorice, I knew. I just knew.

But Mom was right about something. This was the police's responsibility. What was I going to do? Trudge over to wherever she lived and do a citizen's arrest? Call Katie and....

Katie.

If I was right, then Katie might have a lot more to worry about than Lois being codependent.

Despite my surety, as I pulled out my cell to call Branson, I couldn't help but feel foolish. The sensation increased as he answered the phone. "Fred, how are you?"

It took me a second to respond as I realized he must've saved my number in his phone. I decided not to read into that. And again, not important and not the point. "Hear me out." I opted to skip pleasantries so I wouldn't lose my nerve. "I know who killed Opal."

There was silence on the other end of the line. When he spoke, Branson seemed hesitant. "You do?"

"Yeah, I do." I stopped pacing and stood still, closing my eyes even as I worked through it again.

"The morning Watson and I found Opal's body, it was because of these little licorice candies. Watson found them outside the kitchen door, and that's when I went in and found her body. They were scattered across the floor in there as well."

"What—"

I barged on, knowing that if I paused, I might not have the chance to get it all out. "It turns out Opal never made licorice candy. Only Lois. And Lois claims that she never knew Opal was operating an edibles business, or even that she was cooking in Sid's old shop. So what were the licorice candies doing in that kitchen?"

Once again, if I expected a barrage of trumpets of understanding at the end of my spiel, I was sorely disappointed. "So... you believe that Lois killed Opal because some of her licorice candies were at the crime scene?"

From the tone of his voice, I knew I was wasting my time. "Yes."

"Why couldn't Opal have had some of Lois's candy with her? Maybe she liked it."

"Opal didn't like anything Lois made." Even as I said it, I still wasn't sure whether I'd actually heard someone claim that or if it was just my gut instinct.

"Fred...." Branson's sigh didn't sound irritated,

but it felt like he had shifted to speaking to a small child. "I know your dad was a great detective. And I know you're a brave, intelligent woman. But I think you might be in a little over your head here." His voice brightened somewhat. "I thought you'd be glad your stepfather is no longer a suspect."

"I am!" Stupidly I tried again, remembering one of my other points. "What about the murder scenes? They're completely different. You saw them. Opal was hit with a rolling pin and was splayed out over the floor. It was messy. Eddie was shot in the back of the head, and his body was... I don't know, different somehow. How do you explain that?"

"I didn't see Eddie's body. Lyons is in a different county than Estes Park. However, I've seen the pictures and read the report." He was back to sounding like he was explaining things to a child. "Though the weapon might be different, it's very clear the murders are connected. These two individuals were dealing drugs illegally. They had a direct connection and a hostile relationship. Their being killed within days of each other is not a coincidence, Fred. Or did Lois kill Eddie too?"

"I don't know! Maybe?" My temper was getting the best of me. "No, I don't think so. Not that I know Lois, but I don't know why she would kill Eddie."

Branson's tone softened into a kind of soft pity, which only irritated me more. "Why would she kill Opal?"

"I don't think she knew about Opal and Sid dating. It turns out that Lois is a little bit possessive."

"Sid died months ago, Fred."

Oh, right. I kept forgetting that part. "I don't know the motive, all right. But my gut tells me Lois did it. And the clues point that way as well. The licorice candy was right there. Lois's licorice candy."

He sighed again. "Okay, I'll... look into it."

I knew that tone. I'd used that tone countless times. When speaking to an agent, sometimes directly to an author, as I tried to tell them I wasn't interested in the manuscript but they couldn't take no for an answer. That placating "I'll look into it, I'll consider it, I'll give it another try." Everyone knew it was hogwash, but it was polite and made all parties feel better. Kinda.

"Thanks. I appreciate it." I disconnected the call before Branson could say anything else. Before *I* could say anything else. I knew he was just doing his job, and I knew there was a low chance he believed my theory; even my family dismissed it. But still.... If we kept talking, I'd say something I'd regret.

Well, he could think what he wanted. I wasn't

sure how I was going to prove my theory, but I would. It was past being about Barry now. Some part of me knew I should at least claim it was justice for Opal that drove me, but it wasn't. Not really. I wanted to solve this. Needed to. Probably for a bunch of reasons, but I didn't bother to try to figure them out.

I looked around the shop. I was antsy. I needed to do something with my hands. But nothing else needed to be done, and I'd kept the rest of the family waiting long enough for dinner. I spent a few minutes scratching behind Watson's ears, so long that he rolled over, demanding belly rubs. As always, by the time I was finished, we both felt better. Calmer. I didn't have to take care of anything else at this moment. And Lord knew, if I tried, I'd do something rash.

I locked up the shop, and Watson and I started toward the car. Before I made it five feet, I noticed light coming from the back of Healthy Delights.

I paused, considering. Maybe a light had been left on, though I didn't remember noticing it before, but it had still been daylight when we'd started cleaning. Maybe it was Katie, stealing some time away from Lois, though I doubted she would do it there of all places. Maybe Lois?

Maybe Lois.

And at that possibility, all other thoughts fled. In the back my mind, I could feel the tingle of *What are you doing? Do you really think you're going to get her to confess? What do you do if she does?* But they were fuzzy and easy to ignore.

I walked right up to the door and knocked.

There was no answer, no movement inside. I knocked again.

Still nothing.

Maybe the light had been left on from another time and no one was there. Even so, I knocked one more time. There was a shadow in the back, and then a small form emerged and walked through the store. Even silhouetted, it was clearly Lois. As she drew nearer, my blood began to pound in my ears. I focused on remaining calm. As far as Lois knew, there was no reason for me to suspect her.

Lois leaned close to the glass, the streetlights illuminating her face. After a second, she brightened in recognition. With a twist of the lock, she threw open the door.

"Well, Fred! Watson! What a pleasant surprise." Her eyes narrowed, but not in a sinister way as much as I tried to imagine it. "What are you two doing here? It's freezing outside."

I went with the truth. It was simple and relaxed me. "I was just next door getting things ready. We're going to have the refinisher come soon for the floors. Then I noticed a light on in the back of your shop as we were walking to the car. I thought I'd make sure everything was all right."

"Oh, yes dear. I wanted to do some baking this evening. It soothes my soul, you know?" She relaxed a little more. "I so appreciate you checking on me, and my shop. But all is fine."

I could hear the dismissal in her voice. In another second she'd bid me good night and lock the door. I couldn't let that happen, even though I still had no idea what I was doing. I'd just landed on asking Lois for a dog treat for Watson as an excuse to come in when Lois saved me the trouble.

"Actually, Fred, I hate to be an inconvenience, but Katie's been coming down here with me when I bake. Helping me sometimes. She said she didn't have it in her this evening. Her words. So she stayed home. I think she's growing tired of me already." Her eyes grew hopeful. "Would you like to come in for a bit?"

I hesitated for a heartbeat, asking myself if I was truly going to do this, even though I already knew the answer. "Of course. Maybe you can show me the secret to those dog bones Watson loves so much."

Lois stepped back from the door, making room for me even as she shook her head. "I'm sorry, dear. I'm sure it sounds completely awful of me, but I never share recipes. Although I allow people to watch. But I'm not making those this evening, I'm afraid. Tonight is apricot-and-prune brownies. I use them as binding agents for the flour and chocolate. As you know, I only cook vegan, so there's no eggs or milk. But the apricots are a spot of brightness and the prunes give a nice tang."

I could use that sentence alone as evidence that she had the soul of a murderer. "Sounds.... I'd love to... see you in action."

"Wonderful! I'm so glad!"

After she locked the door, Watson and I followed her back into the kitchen. As dog friendly as Estes Park was, I expected her to make a comment about him being where she cooked. She didn't. Instead she gave him one of her massive dog treats.

Now that we were back in her kitchen, my common sense began to scream at me. If I truly believed Lois was the murderer, what in the world was I doing alone with her away from the sight of anyone else? And I was putting Watson in danger as well. Though, I could picture Lois as a murderer, I couldn't imagine her hurting an animal. Surely a vegan wouldn't kill a dog. But even if I was right, even if she was the murderer, I was at least five times stronger than Lois, easily. A stiff breeze was stronger than Lois. Unless she really was Eddie's murderer as well and there was a gun lying about. I couldn't think about that. I'd made my choice. Time to see it through.

Lois returned to her so-called brownies, which were currently a brown glob in the bottom of her mixing bowl. As she started to work, her conversation turned back to Katie. "It's lovely to have you here, Fred. You're such a bright, warm addition to Estes Park. I'm so glad we get to be neighbors." She cast narrowed eyes on me, the kind that told me to keep secrets. "I have a confession. I'm considering having Katie take over my sister's shop. She's been just the sweetest thing since Opal died. Or at least I thought. But she seems to be pulling away. So I'm not sure. We'll have to see how the next few days play out." She gave an apologetic shrug. "I know the girl is desperate for her own bakery, and she has talent. Just like Opal, she uses too much sugar and animal byproducts, but there's talent there. I think I can mold it into something truly wonderful. But I don't see the sense in being neighbors and sharing a lease with someone who looks for excuses to have time away."

Despite knowing it would be best to simply agree with everything Lois said, I couldn't help but defend my friend. "I think Katie would be a wonderful person to pass on the legacy of Opal's baking skills. I'm sure she'd do a fine job."

Lois tossed some sort of seeds into the brownie mixture and nodded at me as if I'd hit the nail on the head. "That's just it. Katie wants her own bakery. She won't recreate Opal's legacy. I need someone who will follow Opal's recipes exactly. Nothing on the menu needs changing. It should stay exactly as it was. I thought Katie was that person. That she could step into the place Opal left behind in the shop."

Intense little lamb was right. I decided to push. "And maybe into the place Opal left behind in your home too?"

"Yes. Exactly." Lois nodded and actually looked relieved that I understood. Giving no hint of awareness of how morbid that truly sounded, she brightened. "I'm so glad you understand. Katie just doesn't seem to." She paused in her movements and turned to me, a new light in her eyes. "Fred, do you bake?"

"No." I did, not at all to Katie's standards, but I wasn't going to say so to Lois.

The look of disappointment barely lasted three seconds. "That's okay. I can teach you. Honestly, Opal's more traditional way of baking is much simpler. You could take over her shop. We can even expand into Heads and Tails. You and Watson could live with me. It would be beautiful."

Now my skin truly did crawl. How Katie had managed one night in the same house as this woman was beyond me. She seemed to transform from a sweet little woman to Norman Bates in a long wig and a dress. But this was definitely the rabbit trail to follow if I planned on getting the confession out of her. But what good would a confession do if it was her word against mine? I really should have thought this through. "Well... I was considering what to do with the top floor of the shop. You... might be onto something."

She almost looked pretty and innocent in her delight. "I knew I liked you." Lois motioned me over. "Come here. Let's finish this recipe together."

My phone. Somehow, if I could get it out and hit the Record button. Did the phone have a Record button? I'd never been great with technology. Maybe if I made a video. I could hit Record on the video and then put it back in the pocket of my skirt. Now how to do that without Lois noticing....

I joined Lois at the mixer. She scooped up a small spoonful and held it out to me. "Here. Taste."

I started to decline but thought better of it, so I reached for the spoon.

She held it away from me. "No, taste."

Nearly feeling violated, I lowered my hand and opened my mouth.

When Lois spoon-fed me the mixture, it took every ounce of my willpower not to shudder, both at the disgusting flavor and texture of the brownie batter and at the sensation of being fed by Lois. I forced a swallow, then a smile. "Very good."

"Thank you. See, you don't need to have sugar to make things sweet. I don't like things unnaturally sweet." She inspected me for a second. "What do you think? Could it use more honey?"

It ought to be thrown in the garbage. "No. I think what you've done is perfect." And I could really use a hot shower.

"I agree." Her smile let me know I'd said the right answer. "I'm so glad you stopped by tonight. It clarified what I was feeling, but didn't want to admit. I've been debating with myself on what to do about Katie. She's constantly making suggestions every night when I'm here baking. As much as I missed her company this evening, it was nice not being told how to improve on my creations." She looked at me ador-ingly. "And now I know why things didn't feel right. You're a godsend, Fred." She started to turn back to the brownie mixture, then narrowed her eyes at me once more. This time there was no illusion of kind-ness there. "You're single, right? No husband or boyfriend?"

I shook my head.

"Are you hoping to find one later?"

"No. I've been down that road. I think I'm done." Even though I was doing nothing more than playing a role at this point, Branson flitted through my mind. "Definitely done." Leo flitted through next.

Good grief.

"Smart girl. That's how it should be. Glad I don't have to worry about that."

I knew it. I knew that was why she'd killed Opal. Even if it had been months after Sid passed. I regretted not having had the time to figure out how to record the conversation on my phone, but there was no time like the present. "I imagine it was hard for you when Opal started dating Sid, wasn't it?"

She stiffened slightly. Then kept right on going. "No. Men were Opal's weakness. She had horrible taste in men. Sid was no surprise. He wasn't any better or any worse than the losers that came before. And he didn't last any longer than the others." She handed me a lemon. "Here, let me get you the juicer. Will you do this for me? Pushing it always hurts my hands."

The switch was so abrupt that it threw me off. "Sure. Of course."

"Thank you, dear. You'll need to cut it in half first."

I retrieved a cutting board from beside the nearby sink. Lois's words replayed through my mind. *Didn't last any longer than the others.* Did that mean...? Maybe I could get her to expand on that. "You weren't a huge fan of Sid, huh? I suppose it makes sense, with him being a taxidermist and all. It seems being a vegan, you would have a problem with—"

I turned to look at her just in time to see her swinging the heavy glass juicer up toward my head. But not soon enough, as it crashed into my temple.

SIXTEEN

My head throbbed, and when I attempted to open my eyes, the bright light of the kitchen caused me to groan. Something wet wiped across my face.

"Goodness. You weren't out very long."

Despite the pain, I blinked several times and forced my eyes open. Watson's black nose was all I could see as he whimpered and licked my face.

Then the picture came into view. I was lying on the kitchen floor. I started to attempt to stand, but something held my hands behind my back.

Lois stood behind Watson, glaring down at me. "You are such a disappointment, Fred. I've heard about the way you and that policeman look at each other. I wondered. Even when you showed up here tonight, I wondered. But you had me convinced, for a few minutes; you really did." She gave a bitter laugh. "To think you could ever replace my sister." She took a step toward Watson, a knife in her hand catching a glint in the light.

I tried to move him aside with my head, but he just licked more ferociously. "Please don't hurt him. Please, Lois."

"How dare you?" Lois halted, looking scandalized. "I would never hurt your dog. Watson hasn't done anything wrong."

Insane or not, relief washed through me. "Thank you." Then I noticed the knife again, and all semblance of gratefulness vanished. I flinched as she stepped toward us again.

"Oh, stop that." She sounded irritated, not at all the gentle tone I'd heard from her up till now. "I'm not going to kill you. At least not here. I learned that with Opal. I wasn't strong enough to move her. I was still trying to figure out what I was going to do with her body when you found her. I'm not going to make that mistake again. That's why I didn't tie your feet. We'll go somewhere else."

I relaxed somewhat at that. I couldn't tell what my hands were tied with, but there was no wiggle room. Lois had done a good job. But if my feet weren't tied. It should be easy.

Why waste time? I whipped my body around, attempting to knock her legs out from under her with my right foot, but only succeeded in sending Watson scrambling away and partially flipping myself over to my stomach.

"Such a disappointment, Fred. I'm not an idiot." Even so, Lois took a step back, still clutching the knife. "Do sit up, dear. There's no need to drag this on."

I rocked, managing to get back on my side, then cast a glance down at my feet. Though not bound together, they were each tied with an extension cord that left only a few inches of slack between them. Enough to shuffle along but not enough to run or kick.

"We don't have all night, so move it along. Sit up." She considered. "Maybe we have all night, but I doubt it. I've learned not to take time for granted."

I lay there, still trying to figure out a new course of action.

"I said sit up!" Lois let out a scream as she stomped her foot.

The way the knife trembled in her hand, I wasn't certain how in control she really was. She might change her mind about Watson, or change her mind about needing to get me somewhere else. And she was right about time. I needed as much of it as I could get.

Not wanting to push her any further, I sat up, making a much greater show of it being difficult than it actually was. Hoping I could use that for when she told me to stand. Give me the time when it happened to look for any chance of attack. With as birdlike as she was, it shouldn't be too hard to shove her into a wall hard enough to do some damage, though doing so without tripping over the extension cord or falling into her knife could be a challenge.

She nodded in approval as I finally rose to a seated position.

"Good. Now stand."

She really wasn't wasting time.

Time really was the thing, wasn't it?

How to get more of it....

Countless mysteries I'd read through the years, and just as many submissions to our publishing company, flitted through my mind. It was a trick as old as the first mystery. One even used on Inspector Gadget, for crying out loud. But if it was good enough for all of them....

"So you killed Opal because she was dating Sid?"

If a person can get the killer talking, it was always their downfall. At least in books.

Maybe Lois hadn't read as many mysteries as I had, because she took the bait.

She sneered at me. "No, of course not. I would never kill my sister because of a man. Why would I kill her because she dated those horrible men? That would be stupid."

Despite needing to think of a way out of this, Lois's words ended up distracting me. "You mean *you* killed Sid?"

"Of course I killed Sid. He was taking her away from me."

She said it so nonchalantly, as if it was the simplest, most obvious thing in the world. The man in her sister's life was eating up her sister's time, so he had to die. No, not man... *men.*

"You killed her three husbands too, didn't you?"

Again her look said the answer was obvious. "They were easy. And planned. They weren't as juvenile as what accidentally happened to Opal. Or what is even happening with you right now. Gradual poisoning is not inventive, but it works. Fiddling with a car, a live wire on a wet floor. No cleanup needed at all."

I most definitely hadn't seen that coming. "I can't believe Opal would cover for you."

"She didn't know. Of course she didn't know."

Her watery eyes grew wide and desperate. "But she would've. If Opal had known, and I was in danger of jail, she would've covered for me. She would have." She waved the knife in my direction. "Now stand up. This isn't a show-and-tell. Get this done." As she spoke, she took a step back. She might be crazy, but she was aware enough to know I wasn't going down without a fight.

And again, I made a show of standing, though it truly was more difficult than sitting up. With my ankles tied so closely together, I had to lean against the wall to push myself to my feet.

And there was no opportunity to attempt anything.

As soon as I was standing, Watson seemed more at ease. He still cast wide eyes in my direction, but he left my side and began to prance around the room in agitation.

"Just to be clear, Fred." Lois waited until I met her gaze. "No funny business. I don't want to, but if it keeps you in line, I will hurt Watson. And if I have to, I'll end you here and now. Figure out how to clean up your mess later."

She meant it. Not that it surprised me at this point, but it was clear there was nothing she wouldn't do. Now that I was standing, my panic rose, and I attempted to keep a clear head. There had to be a simple way out of this. She was a frail old woman. But one who was obviously insane. One who had already killed at least five people. Keep her talking. Just keep her talking. "Why did you kill Eddie?"

She flinched, and for the first time since I'd awoken on the floor, she looked like Lois again. "Who?"

"The owner of Green Munchies?"

Her confusion was genuine.

"The dispensary in Lyons. Where Sid and Opal first got their start to grow their own marijuana plants."

She looked pleased. "I didn't know him, but serves him right. Corrupting my sister that way. I'm glad he got what was coming to him. I wish I knew who it was. I'd bring them a candy basket."

I'd known whoever killed Eddie was different from the person who had killed Opal.

Watson was still skittering around, darting between me, Lois, and the front of the shop. He stood in the doorway of the kitchen, staring at me and whining.

Lois wheeled on him. "Be still, Watson. Be a good boy. I don't want to hurt you, but I can't have you getting loud." I'd just started to attempt a step toward her but halted when she whipped back around to me. "And you, enough of this." She motioned toward the back door with the knife. "Get moving."

I took a few shuffling steps. Watson hurried to my side, then paused. Time. I still needed time. "Then why Opal? If you didn't kill her because of Sid? Then why?"

Despite Lois's desperation to get me moving, her lips snarled at my question, hurt and anger crossing her features. "I never meant to kill Opal. She was my sister. My world. I just...." A tear ran down her cheek, and she wiped at it with the back of her hand, the knife coming dangerously close to her forehead.

Watson went back to the doorway of the kitchen, trying desperately to get me to follow him.

More tears made their way down Lois's cheeks as she glared at me. "I assumed she had a new man. She was sneaking off every night. She thought I didn't know, but I did. So I finally followed her. Followed her right into Sid's shop and up to that kitchen. I confronted her. And she admitted it all. What Sid had introduced her to, how she had turned it from the crackpot idea he'd had to the full business it became. How she'd made a small fortune from those poor dead animals Sid had left behind, and never shared it with me. And the whole time she was talking, she just kept packing. Just packing and packing, because you were in town and going to take over the shop. Telling me I should be glad, that it was helping keep my store afloat." Lois's cadence grew more frantic. "I tried to talk her into letting me be part of it. We could do the cooking right there." She gestured around the kitchen with the knife. "If anything, it would make more sense to come from me. That the business would really take off with my all-natural recipes. She just laughed. I didn't mean to hit her. I really didn't." Even as she shook the knife at me, her expression and tone begged for my understanding, for my forgiveness. "I would never hurt Opal. But she was laughing. At the idea of me making her business better. Not even caring that she'd kept this whole part of her life a secret. That she left me out of it."

The tears had become rivers, and she wiped across her eyes again.

As the time-tested ploy of buying time proved true, I saw my chance. With the knife lifted to her own face, and Watson scurrying back toward me from the kitchen doorway, just behind the back of Lois's feet at the exact right moment, I launched myself toward her. Springing, I smashed into her chest with my shoulders. At the force of my impact, she stumbled back and fell over Watson, who let out a high-pitched yelp, and we crashed to the floor.

I landed on my right shoulder, the pain taking my breath away and causing my vision to go white. I blinked quickly, trying to scurry backward.

But there was no hurry. Lois had hit her head on the counter, or something, on the way down. Her eyes were closed, and the small pool of blood was already growing beneath her head.

Dead. I'd killed her.

There was a flash of panic, a wave of guilt, but I shoved both away.

This time, standing up was harder. Between the pain in my shoulder and my feet getting caught on the hem of my skirt, it took considerable effort. Watson was back at my ankles, whimpering like he was in trouble.

I started to soothe him, but heard a jingle and the scrape of metal at the back door. I attempted to shuffle into the main room, to try to make a run for it. Though, who I was running from, I couldn't say.

Before I'd managed even a step, the door swung open, and Katie stepped inside. "Lois, I'm sorry. I feel horrible, and I shouldn't have—"

Her words fell away, and her eyes grew huge, staring at Lois bleeding on the floor. Then she looked at me, taking in my tied feet and arms. "Fred! Oh, Fred!"

Without sparing another glance at Lois, Katie rushed into the kitchen and began to untie me.

"Fred! What in the world? Are you okay? What's going on?"

With my hands untied, I motioned toward Lois and bent to work on my legs. "Check on her. Is she dead?"

Katie only hesitated for a moment before going to Lois and kneeling. She paused one more second, then pressed two fingers to her throat. A heartbeat passed and then another. She looked up at me. "She's not dead. There's a pulse."

"Thank God!" I nearly sank back to the floor in relief, then refocused on Katie. "Call 911, will you?"

I watched through the window of Healthy Delights as Lois was strapped to a gurney and wheeled through the front doors toward an ambulance. She still hadn't regained consciousness.

Branson raked a large hand through his thick dark hair and shook his head at me. "You are something, Fred Page."

As irritated as I'd been with him earlier, I had to admit I thought the same about him. He'd shown up mere minutes after the first two police cars. He'd clearly been off duty, as he wore a sweater, jeans, and snow boots. He'd stepped in and taken charge, the whole time keeping a protective hand on my shoulder or a watchful eye over me as he spoke to the others.

I glanced over at Katie and handed her my cell. "Would you call my mom? Fill her in on what happened and let her know you'll be joining us for dinner."

"Sure thing." She gave a knowing glance toward Branson, took the phone, and walked away.

Turning back to Branson, try as I might, I couldn't keep the *I told you so* out of my tone. "I told you it was all about the licorice candy." It seemed the *I told you so* wasn't only in my tone.

"That you did." He grinned, started to reach for my hand, but then seemed to think better of it. "I'm sorry about that. It appears I should have given your gut feeling a little more credence."

"Remember that in the future."

His brows shot up. "Do I need to? Is there another murder you're plotting to solve?"

"No." Just the thought made my stomach clench. I narrowed my eyes at him. "But what about Eddie? You thought he and Opal were connected. But Lois genuinely didn't seem to know who he was."

"I was wrong." He shrugged. "I guess they weren't connected. But now that they're not, I really won't be on the case at all, since Eddie isn't part of Larimer County. But I've heard they already have a suspect in his murder." This time his eyes narrowed. "Fred, even if they didn't, you can't go investigating Eddie's death. This was enough."

I liked his protective nature, and I also appreciated how quick he was to say he was wrong and apologize. Again, it set him apart from my ex-husband and more into the category of my father and Barry. But still....

I poked him in the chest. "Maybe you haven't caught on, Sergeant Wexler, but I don't like being told what to do. In the future you might remember that, or I promise you won't find a quicker way to solve a case."

He threw back his head and laughed, the same full, hearty sound he'd let loose in my kitchen. It did things to my heart I would rather it not do. When he looked back, his green eyes were bright and full of affection.

"Noted. Don't tell Fred what to do. Got it." His smile changed slightly. "As a demonstration of that, may I request you reconsider and go to the hospital? If you don't want to take the ambulance, I can drive you."

I started to argue, but the throbbing in my head let me know I was being stubborn for a stupid reason. "I'll ask Katie to take me before we go to my mom's for dinner."

I glanced down at Watson who blinked up at me from where he sat on my foot. He hadn't moved in probably half an hour. I wouldn't be able to say he wasn't affectionate anymore. I'm not sure why I looked at Watson, maybe asking his permission, hoping he'd tell me to reconsider what I was about to do. I didn't find either in his gaze, just corgi adoration. So I made the decision myself and looked back at Branson.

"Would you like to join us after? For dinner? My mom made her grandmother's enchilada recipe. And I know for a fact she picked up her hatch green chilies from some vendor in the canyon, so it should be good and spicy."

He shook his head, the tickle of disappointment clarifying exactly what I was beginning to feel for Branson. "No, thank you. I think your family has seen enough of the police for a little while." That time he did take my hand. "Rain check? When you feel up to it. Perhaps dinner with just you and me?" He gestured down to Watson with his chin. "And little man too, of course. I know you're a package deal."

I nearly said yes, then shrugged. "We'll have to see, Sergeant. This might've been your one and only chance. Ask me later and find out."

Branson shook his head and gave a forced exasperated eye roll. "You really are something."

. . .

The entire family had demanded to meet Katie and me at the hospital, and by the time I was released with a clean bill of health, Mom had to rewarm the enchiladas, causing them to be unusually dry, but still delicious. With five people I loved surrounding me at the table, and Watson still snuggled at my feet, I felt at ease for the first time in days. And with the aroma of home-cooked food combining with the soft glow of the lights, the gentle background sounds of Christmas carols that Mom always put on before Thanksgiving arrived, and snow falling lazily outside the window, I knew I was home. Truly and completely home.

I stayed up a little longer after Katie and my uncles left, simply needing to be in my mother's presence for a while. The twins were returning with their families in a few days, so I needed to soak up as much solitary Mom time as I could before the grandkids took over. At the doctor's urging, I agreed to stay the night, just to have Mom and Barry near.

The next morning, Barry walked Watson and me out to the car. Mom was still asleep, but I needed to be home. Strange how quickly my grandparents' cabin had become home, even without any of my belongings.

"Hold on for a second, Barry, will you?" After I opened the door and let Watson hop in and over the console to his spot, I leaned inside and reached under the passenger seat.

When I handed him the black box tied with a green ribbon, Barry's gaze grew large and darted back toward the house.

I chuckled. "We both know Mom is not going to make a big deal about it. Not really. She might pretend she wasn't aware, but you've known each other since you were kids." I tapped the box. "Consider this a last gift from Eddie. He really did love you."

Barry gave me a long hug, and when he spoke, emotion snagged his voice. "Glad you're all right, kid. I don't know what we would do if anything ever happened to you." He pulled back to look me in the eye. "I only met your dad a couple of times over the years, but with as proud of you as your mom and I are, I can only imagine how proud he'd be of you right now."

And then the emotions were gripping around my throat. I didn't attempt to respond, just squeezed

Barry's shoulder in thanks. Somehow in all the mess of things that night, for the first time since arriving in Estes Park, Dad hadn't entered my mind. How strange. Maybe because I was doing exactly what he would've done. Well, not exactly. I'd made a near mess out of it all at the end, but still....

Barry's typical wacky smile returned, and he kept his voice low. "I might know your mom is okay with this"—he shook the box gently—"and you might know that your mom is okay with this. But that doesn't mean your mom knows she's okay with this."

"It'll be our little secret." I gave him a wink.

My shoulder, neck, and head ached something fierce, but after a hot shower and a few pain pills, it was manageable. If I hadn't already booked an appointment to have the internet hooked up at the Cozy Corgi, I would've crawled into my own bed and slept a couple of hours. Why they could get it to the shop two days earlier than they were willing to schedule it at my cabin, I had no idea. One more thing I decided I would chalk up to small-town life. But as it was, it felt good to get up and move. It wasn't like there was anything to do yet. My things from Kansas City wouldn't be delivered for a while, so I had nothing to do at the house. At least with the internet working at the shop, I could get my first inventory order in. The whole store wouldn't be murder mysteries, but my first order most definitely was going to be nothing but.

I paused as Watson and I walked from the car to the store, and I stared into the window of Healthy Delights. Who would've thought? I gave a little shudder and then spared a glance toward Sinful Bites. I supposed I'd have new neighbors. Hopefully they wouldn't be killers. Another thought hit me and warmed my heart a little. Maybe Katie would get her bakery, after all. It would be lovely having her next door.

Barely ten minutes passed before there was a knock. Watson barked more hysterically than normal. Probably a little traumatized from the night before.

We made our way back downstairs when there was another knock. I could see a man in uniform outside the glass front door. Surprise, surprise, apparently there were some advantages to small-town life. You'd never get an internet provider showing up early in the city.

When I opened it, I realized my mistake. Not the internet provider. Instead a cute young man with his brown delivery uniform showing between the folds of his jacket. He held out a tablet. "If you'll just sign this, I'll bring your delivery inside. It's heavy."

One look at the large box, and I knew what it was. My heart began to beat like mad. I scribbled my name and thrust the tablet back into his hands. "Thank you so much! Have a good day." Then I practically shoved him out the door.

As I began to rip open the box, I gave Watson what was probably the most foolish of smiles. "Wait until you see this. I ordered it last week before we headed out."

Despite all the cleaning we'd done the day before, I ripped into it like it was Christmas morning, chunks of cardboard flying and packing peanuts acting like snow.

With a grunt, I pulled the huge wooden board free. The deliveryman had been right. The thing was a heavy beast. Which was good. It was quality. At least it better be, considering what I'd paid for it.

After ripping off the final layer of plastic, I inspected it and let out a happy sigh of satisfaction. The edges of the wood were scrolled so they made the outline of an open book. The interior had been painted white but artistically aged, and arching blue letters near the top of it read: *The Cozy Corgi.*

Beneath the letters, in the same aged blue, was a stack of books with a corgi sitting on the top. It was perfect.

I angled the sign so Watson could see. "What do you think? It's you!"

Watson leaned warily closer, and gave a little sniff. Some of the packing pieces went flying, and he shook his head. Then he inspected once more, and there was a furrow between his eyes as he studied the corgi.

He didn't like it.

"I know he's a little bit fatter... er... fluffier than you, but I thought it made him cute." I tapped the chubby corgi sitting on the books. "Let's be honest. With the amount of dog treats you've been getting lately, this silhouette is only a matter of days away."

And at that word, that magical, ridiculous, annoying word, Watson's displeasure disappeared and he began to pounce on his front paws.

I sighed. "If you are anything, Watson Page, you're predictable." I leaned the heavy sign against the wall, then motioned toward the door. "Well, come on. I'm sure I have some treats in the car."

TWISTER SISTERS MYSTERIES

COMING EARLY 2022

I can't begin to tell you how excited I am to finally bring this series to life. It's been in the planning and dreaming stages for over three years. The process was interrupted by my cancer diagnosis and all that came with it. A blessing in disguise, as the characters have kept me company over these years and have grown richer, deeper, and are producing a limited series (10 books in total) that is so much better than if things had gone according to *my* plan.

The Twister Sisters takes place in the charming Ozark town of Willow Lane. You've actually already met our three lead characters in the knitting group that crashed Percival and Gary's anniversary at Baldpate Inn in *Killer Keys* (the book where Fred and Leo shared their first kiss)!

You'll follow along with Cordelia, Wanda, and Pamela as they deliver their casseroles (Meals-on-Wheels style) and just happen to... you guessed it... solve murders!

The first three books are already up for pre-order, so you don't have to worry about missing their arrival!

And... this doesn't mean the end for the Cozy Corgi. Trust me, Fred—and even Watson—are cheering on their friends in their new adventure.

While Twister Sisters is a limited series, the Cozy Corgi is not. There's plenty of shenanigans ahead for our Scooby Gang.

Twister Sisters Mysteries

Katie's Shortbread Lemon Bar recipe provided by:

2716 Welton St Denver, CO 80205

(720) 708-3026

Click the links for more Rolling Pin deliciousness:

RollingPinBakeshop.com

Rolling Pin Facebook Page

Katie's Shortbread Lemon Bars

Crust:

1/2 cup butter

1/4 cup powdered sugar

1 cup flour

Filling:

2 eggs

1 cup sugar

2 T lemon juice

Zest from 1 lemon

2 teaspoons flour

1/2 teaspoon baking powder

1/4 teaspoon salt

1. Preheat oven to 350 degrees. Cream butter and powdered sugar. Stir in flour and spread the mixture over the bottom of an 8 X 8 cake pan and pat down. Bake 10 to 12 minutes or until lightly browned.

2. While crust is baking, prepare lemon filling. Lightly beat eggs, then stir in sugar, lemon juice and lemon zest. Stir together flour, baking powder and salt. Stir into egg mixture. As soon as the crust is done baking, pour mixture over the crust. Put it back in the oven and bake until the filling is set and just beginning to brown. About 20 to 25 minutes. Put the pan on a rack and when completely cooled, cut into squares. Remove the lemon bars from the pan and sprinkle them with powdered sugar.

PATREON

Mildred Abbott's Patreon Page

Mildred Abbott is now on Patreon! By becoming a member, you gain access to exclusive Cozy Corgi merchandise, get a look behind the scenes of book creation, and receive real-life writing updates, plans, and puppy photos (becuase, of course there will be puppy photos!). You can also gain access to ebooks and recipes before publication, read future works *literally* as they are being written chapter by chapter, and can even choose to become a character in one of the novels!

Wether you choose to be a villager, busybody, police officer, super sleuth, or the fuzzy four-legged star of the show himself, please come check the

Mildred Abbott Patreon community and discover what fun awaits.

Personal Note: Being an indie writer means that some months bills are paid without much stress, while other months threaten the ability to continue the dream of writing. Becoming a member ensures that there will continue to be new Mildred Abbott books. Your support is unbelievably appreciated and invaluable.

*While there are many perks to becoming a patron, if you are a reader who can't afford to support (or simply don't feel led), rest assured you will *not* miss out on any writing. All books will continue to be published just as they always have been. None of the Mildred Abbott books will become exclusive to a select few. In fact, patrons help ensure that writing will continue to be published for everyone.

Mildred Abbott's Patreon Page

AUTHOR NOTE

Dear Reader:

Thank you so much for reading *Cruel Candy*. If you enjoyed Fred and Watson's adventure, I would greatly appreciate a review on Amazon and Goodreads. Please drop me a note on Facebook or on my website (MildredAbbott.com) whenever you like. I'd love to hear from you.

And don't miss book two, Traitorous Toys, coming out this Christmas. Keeping turning the page for sneak peek!

Much love, Mildred

PS: I'd also love it if you signed up for my newsletter. That way you'll never miss a new release. You won't hear from me more than once a month, nobody needs that many newsletters!

Newsletter link: Mildred Abbott Newsletter Signup

ACKNOWLEDGMENTS

A special thanks to Agatha Frost, who gave her blessing and her wisdom. If you haven't already, you simply MUST read Agatha's Peridale Cafe Cozy Mystery series. They are absolute perfection.

The biggest and most heartfelt gratitude to Katie Pizzolato, for her belief in my writing career and being the inspiration for the character of the same name in this series. Thanks to you, Katie, our beloved baker, has completely stolen both mine and Fred's heart!

Desi, I couldn't imagine an adventure without you by my side. A.J. Corza, you have given me the corgi covers of my dreams. A huge, huge thank you to all of the lovely souls who proofread the ARC versions of Cruel Candy and helped me look somewhat literate (in completely random order): Ann Attwood, Meghan Maslow, Melissa Brus, Cinnamon, Janie Beaton, Kristell Harmse, Ron Perry, Rob Andresen-Tenace, Terri Grooms, Michael Bailey, Kelly Miller, TL Travis, Jill Wexler, Patrice, Lucy Campbell, Chris Dancer, Natalie Rivieccio, A.C. Mink, Rebecca Cartee, Becca Waldrop, and Sue Paulsen. Thank you all, so very, very much!

A further and special thanks to some of my dear readers and friends who support my passion: Andrea Johnson, Fiona Wilson, Katie Pizzolato, Maggie Johnson, Marcia Gleason, Rob Andresen- Tenace, Robert Winter, Jason R., Victoria Smiser, Kristi Browning, and those of you who wanted to remain anonymous. You make a huge, huge difference in my life and in my ability to continue to write. I'm humbled and grateful beyond belief! So much love to you all!

Chattering Chipmunks

Vengeful Vellum

Wretched Wool

Jaded Jewels

Yowling Yetis

Lethal Lace

Book 24 (*untitled*) - Summer 2022

(Books 1-10 are also available in audiobook format, read to perfection by Angie Hickman.)

-the Twister Sisters Mystery Series-

Starting early 2022

Hippie Wagon Homicide

Casserole Casualty

Bandstand Bloodshed

-Cozy Corgi Merchandise-

now available at:

the Cozy Corgi store at Cafe Press